*"Maybe y***...**down a little more,"* Jonas said.

"G-Man, that's what got me in this condition." Lifting her gaze to meet his, Alyx added, "And look who's talking—Mr. Ask Me No Questions So I Don't Have To Spin Tall Tales."

"I don't recall you asking me anything that I couldn't answer," Jonas said.

"That's because I wasn't interested in classified information," she countered.

"Why do you think I made all those trips down to Austin?" he asked.

"You said you were working on cases."

"Over holidays? C'mon, Alyx. We spent every spare minute you had together. Didn't that give you a clue to how I felt?"

In the reverberating silence Jonas suspected he'd gone too far. Sometimes there was nothing left to do but cut to the important thing. Clasping his hand to the back of her head, he claimed her mouth with his.

Dear Reader,

Two characters that lingered in my mind from my last Special Edition novel, *A Man to Count On,* were Alyx Carmel, the divorce attorney and friend of heroine E. D. Martel, and FBI Special Agent Jonas Hunter, an old school friend of the hero, Judge Dylan Justiss. It was clear from the start that there was chemistry between Alyx and Jonas, but aside from their irresistible physical attraction, it seemed we were dealing with an oil-and-vinegar couple.

The more I thought about this couple the more I saw parallels to Elizabeth Bennett and Mr. Darcy in Jane Austen's *Pride and Prejudice.* Both Alyx and Jonas have great professional pride and their perceptions of each other are weakly based on minimal information and experience. As fate would have it, the more they're resolved not to reexamine those faulty perceptions, the more their paths cross, until they can't help but be forced into seeing that while they differ on surface issues, they share important qualities and values that, given the chance, could enhance the passion they otherwise bring out in each other.

I hope you enjoy their journey of discovery and love, and as always, thank you for reading.

Warm regards,

Helen

THE LAST MAN SHE'D MARRY

HELEN R. MYERS

SPECIAL EDITION

Published by Silhouette Books

America's Publisher of Contemporary Romance

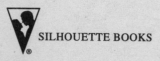 SILHOUETTE BOOKS

ISBN-13: 978-0-373-24914-5
ISBN-10:   0-373-24914-4

THE LAST MAN SHE'D MARRY

Copyright © 2008 by Helen R. Myers

Visit Silhouette Books at www.eHarlequin.com

Printed in U.S.A.

Books by Helen R. Myers

Silhouette Special Edition

After That Night... #1066
Beloved Mercenary #1162
What Should Have Been #1758
A Man To Count On #1830
The Last Man She'd Marry #1914

Silhouette Romance

Donovan's Mermaid #557
Someone To Watch Over Me #643
Confidentially Yours #677
Invitation to a Wedding #737
A Fine Arrangement #776
Through My Eyes #814
Three Little Chaperones #861
Forbidden Passion #908
A Father's Promise #1002
To Wed at Christmas #1049
The Merry Matchmaker #1121
Baby in a Basket #1169

*Daddy Knows Last

Silhouette Books

Silhouette Shadows Collection
"Seawitch"

Montanta Mavericks
The Law Is No Lady #8

Silhouette Desire

Partners for Life #370
Smooth Operator #454
That Fontaine Woman! #471
The Pirate O'Keefe #506
Kiss Me Kate #570
After You #599
When Gabriel Called #650
Navarrone #738
Jake #797
Once Upon a Full Moon #857
The Rebel and the Hero #941
Just a Memory Away #990
*The Officer and the
  Renegade* #1102

Silhouette Shadows

Night Mist #6
Whispers in the Woods #23
Watching for Willa #49

MIRA Books

Come Sundown
More Than You Know
Lost
Dead End
Final Stand
No Sanctuary
While Others Sleep

HELEN R. MYERS,

is a collector of two- and four-legged strays, and lives deep in the Piney Woods of East Texas. She cites cello music and bonsai gardening as favorite relaxation pastimes, and still edits in her sleep—an accident, learned while writing her first book. A bestselling author of diverse themes and focus, she is a three-time RITA® Award nominee, winning for *Navarrone* in 1993.

Chapter One

A bad day wasn't the half of it.

Alyx Carmel didn't speak the words out loud, but the first strains of a current pop tune all but mimicked her as it blared through the audio system of Mesa Rehab-Fitness Center. She clenched her teeth and released the handles of the resistance machine she'd been working on. While the machine swooshed, then thudded to a rest position, she considered hunting down the stereo system, wondering how much it would cost to replace the annoying thing, since she was of a good mind to toss it through the nearest window.

Yes, she was having a bad day, year, *life*. All that was needed to propel her over the edge was another glass-half-full dose of mind-numbing music and she would challenge any court to hold her responsible for her behavior.

"Come on, Alyx, you have to try a little harder."

The girlish voice belonged to none other than blond, ponytailed Sharleigh Moss, a California transplant, who retained the tan to look the part, although by her own admission Shar avoided actual sunlight more than an Ann Rice vampire. Alyx had to admit that the instructor knew her equipment, but her obvious hunt for a man to rescue her from the need of a paycheck was as insulting to Alyx as her voice was annoying.

And one more thing, she fumed to herself without generosity: how could anyone operating a business in a geographic location advertised to be as harmonious and spiritual as Sedona, Arizona, let this fuse-busting lady longlegs run a rehab center like some kind of torture chamber?

Increasingly irritated with the trainer-therapist, who had just excused the man with the barely bandaged knee from finishing his quota of leg pumps, Alyx strained to sit up. "No, actually, I don't have to try harder. I *have* to protect myself because it's clear there's no one else watching out for my well-being but *me*."

Her injuries might not be immediately visible, but if she ripped open the neckline of her T-shirt to look like some cover models, everyone in the room would probably gag. With that certainty embittering her, Alyx pushed away Shar's extended hand and pushed herself to her feet.

"Was that necessary?"

The way she glanced around self-consciously had Alyx wondering. *She's worried about her reputation.* Shaking her head in weariness, she managed civility if not warmth. "I've been trying to tell you that the regimen you devised for me is too much. I can barely drive to the house at the end of the session, let alone function once I get there."

"You've only been at this for a week. It's always difficult in the beginning."

Who cared? Alyx didn't like to test her limits on anything except her mental prowess. The closest she came to being athletic was an occasional soak in a hot tub. Granted, she had started some yoga in the year before the attack, but that was for stress relief.

"I'm thirty-nine, not nineteen," she reminded the twenty-something spa employee, "and I'm starting from scratch—just like your *other* clients."

"I know you think I'm giving other *patients* preferential treatment, Alyx. But please consider this—you're late in getting help. Odds are some damage is already permanent, which makes me the automatic bad guy. The harder I push early on, the greater progress we may achieve before fatigue has you seriously locking those mental brakes."

"Good grief, you poor saint. I'll just haul my insensitive self out of here to give you more time with people who are gluttons for punishment."

As she began to rise, Sharleigh signaled caution with a raised hand.

"Look, I can take the sarcasm. In fact, I prefer it to those who kick or bite me. I'm just trying to impress upon you the great mistake it would be to give up." Regaining some of her perkiness, Sharleigh tossed her gloss-enhanced ponytail over one shoulder before crossing her arms under her lemon-yellow sports bra. "Come on, help me out. I have a reputation to protect."

For relief, Alyx visualized a pot of cooked cabbage

dumped over the annoying kid's head. Lukewarm, of course. "You haven't lived long enough to have one."

"Pardon me?"

Once upon a time in a courtroom, Alyx could have rendered Shar mute using a minimum of words. But she'd lost her stomach for those kinds of power plays. Rising, she leaned over and replied in a conspiratorial whisper, "I promise to keep it a secret that you wasted your time on me."

Barely resisting the urge to massage the throbbing ache that ran from shoulder to wrist, Alyx decided her best bet was to head for the lockers and get out of here. A hot shower at the house would keep her from the temptation of popping pills or worse.

It was August now, seven months since the attack that fiercely cold January day in Austin, Texas, that had changed her life forever. Contrary to Shar's opinion, she'd been trying to follow medical advice at home but was beginning to conclude that the pain wasn't worth the lack of results. Her surgeon had been one of the tops in his field and he'd warned her about that, warned that some of the damage done by Doug Conroe, ex of her deceased client Cassandra Field Conroe, would probably be permanent. With her usual survivalist bravado, Alyx had assured him that she would be fine. After all, she was alive, while poor Cassandra was buried back in Austin, Texas; what's more, her work didn't entail anything more physical than carrying briefcases, climbing stairs in high heels, and punching the heck out of a BlackBerry. Considering the hours she billed, she'd told her doctor, she could afford to hire someone to handle everything but her vain commitment to wearing high heels. The doctor refused to be amused, and about ten days ago Alyx had stopped pretending.

She'd walked away from her practice, her home, from everything and almost everyone who had been part of her life. The timing had seemed ordained—her cousin, Parke Preston, an artist whose work graced an increasing number of hotels and restaurants in Sedona and elsewhere in the southwest—had been about to cancel out on an invitation to take a trip to Europe. Parke's dilemma? She had no one to watch her home and beloved dog, a rescued greyhound named Grace. Although Alyx was no animal hugger, she and Grace were getting along better every day. Alyx wished she could have been as enthusiastic about Parke's health club.

Once outside in the blazing Arizona sun, Alyx all but stopped in her tracks. The drier summer air had her wanting a bottle of water. She was used to a more humid environment back in Texas, thanks to the Gulf of Mexico frequently wafting moisture up into southern plains. In this higher elevation, man-size-cactus country, the environment was even less friendly to sweatpants and an oversize T-shirt over a sports bra after the sun rose. But it was her outfit of choice to hide her scars.

Maybe it was time to consider an adjustment, she allowed as she snatched her keys out of her bag and slung the straps over her good shoulder. Yet, although her leg cuts were all but healed, she still woke at night from spasms of pain. The doctor had assured her they were psychosomatic, ghost pains, and would ease in time. She was waiting and wondered—if they were wrong about that, what about the rest of her prognosis? At least she'd managed to wean herself off those tempting and addictive pain pills.

Wanting nothing more than to get to the house and take a soothing shower, she slipped on her sunglasses and nodded her thanks to the driver in a car that stopped to let her cross into the aisle where she'd parked Parke's black SUV. Within minutes, she was at the exit of the strip mall ready to merge with traffic.

As usual, the town was already abuzz with activity, no surprise for such a tourist spot and spiritual haven. While some shops were welcoming early shoppers, many hikers had been well on their way up and down the multitude of trails winding through the valleys and up the cliffs that surrounded the community since before she'd first left the house. The rest—residents and longer-term visitors like herself—strove for patience navigating through all of that. About to zip past a tour bus, Alyx realized she was at the shopping center where Parke had directed her to buy groceries. Ducking back into the right lane, she heard the motorized equivalent of "the finger." She had managed to press another native's patience besides Sharleigh's.

"Sorry, sorry!" Waving and cringing, Alyx turned into the parking lot and found a slot blessedly close to the market. All she had to do was get inside, find the produce section, and sack enough fruits and vegetables to guarantee a two- or three-day break from human contact, she thought. By then, surely she would have regrouped to where she could formulate plan B toward recovery without breaking into a cold sweat.

This time last year such pitiful reasoning would have made her snort "Wimp," in disdain. Alyx Carmel afraid of the public and shunning mirrors? Alyx Carmel a shrinking violet? Her detractors would choke on their martinis in shock.

What a difference a year made.

She all but sighed in ecstasy upon finding the store virtually empty except for some clerks still restocking shelves. Alyx grabbed a red plastic basket instead of a wagon, and maneuvered around the stack of dried fruit to tug free a plastic bag for bananas. No sooner did she reach for a bundle than a strong, hair-covered masculine hand closed over hers.

Alyx recoiled as though stung by a scorpion. "Excuse me—"

"My fault. Guess we have the same good taste."

A sleepy-eyed, whiskered man close to her own five foot eight took a shuffling step back and, offering a jocular smile, bowed with courtly charm for her to continue. "After you."

"I didn't see you," Alyx said, disconcerted by her preoccupation. She could have sworn no one had been nearby, couldn't even use the excuse that her vision had been hampered by sunglasses. She'd removed them the moment she'd nearly had a head-on collision with a soda machine by the entrance of the store.

"That's what I get for charging around like the place was my own backyard," the stranger said with a toss of his unkempt mane. "Go ahead, please. I'd rather watch a beautiful woman any day than deal with a shopping list."

Oh, brother. Even if she hadn't been in this vulnerable mood and he had been washed, never mind drop-dead gorgeous, Alyx would never fall for such a mediocre line. Casting him a thanks-but-no-thanks look, she grabbed at a decent-looking bunch of bananas on the far side of the display.

"There's a bruised one on that," the stranger said, leaning over her shoulder. "The next one behind it is better."

Stiffening against the invasion of her personal space, Alyx hardened her voice. "But more than I wanted."

"Hey, no wedding ring? Me, either," he said, wiggling the fingers of his left hand before her face. "I'm Denny. Put back that crummy bunch and I'll pick you a better one."

"If you'll excuse me, I'm in a hurry." Ignoring his offer, she stepped around the man to get to the tomato display. Unfortunately, Denny soon proved himself to be the type not easily dissuaded.

"They've got decent coffee at the deli," he said close on her heels. "Can I buy you a cup?"

"Thank you, but no."

"Why not? You don't look dressed to where you have to hurry back to work."

Internal alarm bells sounded inside her. That was a subtle put-down if she'd ever heard one, and as a divorce attorney, she'd heard plenty—from personal attacks and from stories told by clients, spouses of masters of passive-aggressive behavior. What a cheap way to make a woman grateful for a man's attention. All it did to Alyx, though, was to remind her of those wounded people she'd tried to help, people who had listened to such drivel for longer than was sane—or safe. Well, this lover boy was about to learn that he had made a poor choice if he was looking for his next doormat.

Giving him her most chilling look, she enunciated, "Let me make this as clear as possible—I. Am. Not. Interested."

He shed her remark like water off a duck's back. Beaming back at her, he asked, "Why not? You look like a nice person. I *know* I'm a nice person."

"Who told you that, your mother? My hunch is she lied to get you to leave the nest."

Denny laughed, but something in his gaze sharpened. "You're tough."

"You don't want to find out how right you are."

Giving him what Alyx hoped was her best courtroom ice-queen look, she snatched a bundle of vine-ripe tomatoes in a net bag. "Lettuce and milk," she muttered to herself. Then she could put this nonsense behind her.

"Aw, now, tell me you aren't a vegetarian?"

Was there a hidden TV camera catching all of this for some silly reality show? Alyx doubted she was that lucky. Either this character was honing some creepy method-acting muscles, or she had a stalker candidate on her hands. "Sir," she intoned, "can you not take a hint?"

"It's nothing to be ashamed about." He shrugged as though she hadn't spoken. "I'm a true-blue beef lover myself, but I can risk turf-and-surf as a change of pace if it means spending the evening with you."

As her scalp started prickling, Alyx knew that if she didn't get out of there, she would be facing a full-fledged panic attack. In desperation she looked for a market employee—naturally, they'd all vanished, either they had gone to different aisles or back into the warehouse for more supplies.

"Okay, Hard Time," she said, turning on the man with grim determination. "Either go away or I call for the manager."

"Shoot, he's my uncle."

It was all she could do not to gape. Why hadn't Parke warned her about this great mental and physical lug? It sounded like this self-anointed Casanova was a regular fixture in the store.

Her cousin was the eye candy: coal-black hair inherited from Welsh ancestors, and piercing black eyes that could hint at a great soul, but didn't apologize for temper when necessary. Truth be known, Alyx had coveted her dramatic coloring when they were kids—her own coloring had been teasingly called Welsh-light—and had emulated Parke more than once during tough cases when the situation warranted the Lone Ranger style of help-or-get-out-of-my-way approach. It had usually worked. She could use a dose of her cousin's verbal strength now.

"Your uncle? What's his name?" When Denny failed to answer, Alyx drew a deep breath and called, "Uncle of *Denny!* You're needed in Produce!"

Denny's smile flattened. "That wasn't funny…or polite."

"Neither is bothering women who don't want your brand of special attention."

She dropped the tomatoes into her basket with less care than they deserved, and strode out of the section; spotting the aisle sign for bread, she veered left. A third of the way down it, she had to sidestep a deliveryman pushing a tiered cart to restock shelves, then she grabbed the first loaf of oat-nut bread she came upon. In the next instant she was gasping with pain as a vise closed around her wounded upper arm and she was swung around.

"No!"

Training as much as instinct had Alyx shoving Denny away from her. Unfortunately, that sent him into the wheel-based tower of fresh bread. She watched in a mixture of fascination and dread as the surprised man triggered an avalanche of plastic trays full of baked goods. Denny ducked and dodged; then, growling with anger, he charged again.

Still swallowing against the pain in her upper arm, Alyx wrapped her good arm around the damaged one and dropped into a tight ball on the linoleum in the hope of escaping further injury. She heard a crash and looked up to see that this time Denny was being fully buried under trays and bread. Had she done that?

"Are you nuts? Hey, mister! Help get him out from under there!"

Blinking, Alyx saw Denny being hoisted by the collar out of the pile of bread and plastic like a scrappy pup, an impressive feat, considering the size of the guy. More amazing was that while her rescuer was taller than Denny, he was leaner—but what a great butt for jeans.

Wait a minute, she thought. *I've had that response before.*

"Get lost," her hero snarled. "Pull that stunt again and so help me, I will drag your sorry backside through every cactus between here and Agave Ground Zero."

Jonas?

Alyx stared in growing horror as the man with the silvering blond hair shoved a dazed Denny the rest of the way out of the aisle. By the time he turned to face her, she didn't need to see his face for confirmation; every angle of him was imprinted in her mind—although her brain was feeling as if she'd just suffered the second concussion of her life.

Passing the slack-jawed deliveryman, Agent Jonas Hunter of the FBI squatted before her. "Are you okay?" he asked, frowning as his gaze swept over her face.

"What are you doing here?" It was a rude response, considering that he'd just rescued her from a guy who had been a serious handful. She should be hugging him with gratitude, but as the pain spasms eased, the one emotion she was aware of was dread, snowballing dread that felt as though it was about to crush her.

"Yeah. Small world." He nodded at where only he knew she hurt and kept his next words low. "Can we get you to your feet and finish this conversation elsewhere? You look like you need fresh air—or a barf bag."

Over his shoulder, Alyx saw that the bread guy was unsure as to whether to offer his assistance to her or run. For his sake more than anything, Alyx allowed Jonas to assist her to her feet.

"I appreciate what you did," she said loud enough for the route salesman to hear.

For his part, Jonas's gaze stayed on her. "Did he reinjure your shoulder? Do you think you need to go to the hospital?"

That rallied her spirit somewhat. "It would take a battalion of marines to get me to another of those," she said with a pointed look. "I can live with a little soreness."

Jonas snorted. "You'd carry your own limb into Emergency and chide the fainting internist for being a weenie."

"Now who's being overly dramatic?"

"Then let me point out there isn't a drop of blood left in your face."

She took a stabilizing breath. "I was startled. Now I'm fine. Speaking of which, where did my basket go?"

"I've got it." He quickly scooped it up from between the trolley and shelves, then switched it to his other hand to keep it out of her reach. "Is there anything else you need? Why don't you go sit in your car? I can finish for you. On second thought, let me escort you outside to make sure that guy isn't waiting around the corner or something."

He was being as considerate and kind as though they'd

had breakfast together this morning and parted with a kiss, when, in fact, they hadn't seen each other in months—seven to be exact. They also hadn't parted well. The fault had been hers, but Alyx didn't want to think about those days again, let alone deal with this. Then she reminded herself that Jonas was being the consummate professional; he wasn't treating her with any special attention, he would do this for anyone.

She gestured for him to give her the basket. "Really, I can take it from here, but thank you for your kindness." When he failed to comply, she stepped closer to take hold of one side and tugged gently. Had she been wrong about him? Well, she couldn't let him prolong this; people were starting to collect at the end of the aisle and stare. "Please, Jonas."

His frown remained quizzical. "Sorry. I'm still trying to get it—what are you doing here?"

He was surprised? So much for her first assumption that this was some kind of a romantic ploy of his making. As embarrassment sent a rush of heat into her cheeks, she scowled back at him and yanked. "You didn't tell me, why should I tell you?" At least the tug succeeded in her taking possession of the basket.

"Stubborn woman." He glanced at the gawkers, then offered a negligible shrug. "I'm helping a friend. Now you?"

"The same—only it's a cousin."

"Weak save."

"Believe me or not, it makes no difference."

He looked instantly regretful for his mockery, touched her arm, and nodded to indicate they should start toward the front of the store. "I want to understand," he said under his breath as he fell in beside her. "I did from the first. You shut me out."

Oh, no more, please. She so wanted not to have this conversation again. "I was doing you a favor. You had a job to get back to."

"I would have been willing to take some extra time off."

He'd never said that. At any rate he didn't have the luxury, *that* much she understood. "You don't have a job, you have a career." There was a vast difference. Men like Jonas put in their twenty-something years with pride and dogged determination regardless of what was asked of them. Dedication wasn't easy to walk away from, and after all of the effort and expense invested in developing an agent, the FBI wouldn't make it easier. What's more, the grim truth was that they'd had a *fling*. A few weekends here and there when he could fly down from Washington, D.C., to Austin, Texas. It was hardly what anyone could have called a relationship. Actually, the one *gift* in all of what had happened—to use the term darkly—was that it had ended before she had to worry that they were, indeed, heading toward some sort of understanding and all that meant.

Her silence had him studying her profile. "You don't believe me about wanting to help you. What did you think all of those calls and notes were about?"

An almost lifelong survival technique triggered her stubbornness and need to be in control. "Maybe I didn't want to be anyone's project." As they came to the express checkout, she handed the basket over to the checker.

"Ma'am...my apologies." The store manager came around the counter to bag. His face was flushed, a stark contrast to his crisp white shirt. "Is there anything that I can do? Are you all right?"

Was this Denny's uncle? Alyx saw no familial resemblance in the meticulously coifed, sandy-haired, anxious man to the big lug who'd accosted her. "I'm fine, thank you." Wanting only escape, she nodded to the basket. "I'd just like to pay for this and go home."

With abject humility, the man gestured toward the door. "Allow me to sack those and please—no charge. I'm sorry you were—that you had this experience. Let me reassure you it won't happen again."

Alyx wondered how often he had to dig into his own pocket to cover for his sister's—or brother's—overgrown delinquent? Feeling bad for him, Alyx said, "I appreciate that, but I don't need you to comp my purchases."

"Where's the guy who assaulted her?" Jonas interjected.

The manager's eyes darted from entrance to entrance before he cleared his throat. "He's—uh—being driven home, sir. And I've called his—his home. His family will see that he stays there."

At another time, Alyx would have smiled that Jonas intimidated him. When she'd first laid eyes upon this friend of Judge Dylan Justiss last year, she'd had to struggle to keep her usual cool decorum, too, and for an instant hadn't been so upset that her client, Deputy DA E. D. Martel, and Dylan were besotted with each other at a most inopportune time. There was something about Jonas's Hollywood good looks that demanded attention as well…who was it he reminded her of?

Audrey Hepburn's pining love interest in *Breakfast at Tiffany's*—George Peppard. After all this time it had finally come to her.

"Here you are, miss." Ignoring her debit card, the manager held her bagged items out to her. "Again, I'm very sorry."

"Thanks." Painfully aware of all the eyes following her, Alyx exited the store as fast as possible, wanting nothing more than to get to Parke's black RAV4. The vehicle was a little "outdoorsy" for her, but it represented escape, which was all that mattered.

"Alyx? A moment?"

With her thumb on the ignition key's computerized lock, she paused. Drawing a deep breath, she turned to face her ex-lover and waited for him to voice whatever he felt this rescue had earned him the right to say. What could it hurt at this point? She might look like a worn-out dishtowel ready for the garbage, but at least there was no media around to extend her embarrassment to the evening news.

Jonas slipped on his sunglasses. Perfect G-man mode, she thought. Seek out secrets, but keep your own.

"No explanation? No nothing?"

His soft-spoken query had an edge to it and she couldn't blame him one bit for being annoyed that "thank you" wasn't enough either personally or professionally. But she, too, was known to be a hard read in her personal life and a barracuda for her clients. So, bottom line, she had no inclination to explain herself today, and might never.

"What's done is done, Jonas. You have your world and I have mine. Let's leave well enough alone." Only when she replaced her own glasses did she risk glancing up at him. Despite the filtered lenses, in the bright sunlight, what she saw brought a bit of a shock. He no longer had that Teflon, nothing-sticks, smooth-operator look that she remembered. His face was sunken, more lined and his mouth had a harder twist.

"'Well enough'?" he snapped, breaking into her thoughts, "Alyx, have you looked in a mirror lately? There may be no blood this time, but you still look one missed depression pill away from suicide." With a muttered expletive, he walked away.

The sting of his criticism, regardless of its accuracy, made it impossible to resist striking back. "Yeah?" she called to his back. "Well, consider the compliment returned and then some!"

Men. Here she was doing him a favor—whether he knew it or not—but leave it to Testosterone Man that when rejected, he was determined to cut her down to manageable size.

Inside her cousin's SUV, Alyx tossed the bag onto the passenger's seat and shoved the key into the ignition. Tried, that is. Her hands were shaking so hard she had to grip her wrist and direct it in. That's when the tears started pouring down her cheeks.

"Crap."

Desperate for the privacy of Parke's house, Alyx blindly ripped at tissues from the box in the console and slipped them under the sunglasses to dab at her eyes. Never would she have suspected that seeing Jonas again would have this effect on her. After the attack, it had been a relief when he'd stopped coming to the hospital and had returned to Washington, D.C., better still when he'd stopped phoning and e-mailing.

Why start all that again when he claimed to be here for a friend? He'd certainly left without too much coercion.

Recovering somewhat, Alyx carefully backed out of the

parking space, but she kept an eye out for Jonas. When she spotted him a lane away climbing into a red vintage Mustang convertible, her caution turned to skepticism, which sent her eyebrows arching.

"The government must be paying well these days if that's what was allowed from the rental counters," she muttered.

Accelerating, she made it to the exit and turned right onto the main road. Parke's house was another few miles west and a bit down from the plateau where the municipal airport was located. At the next traffic light, she eased the SUV left to the turning lane, and it was as she was waiting for the light that she spotted the Mustang two cars behind her.

What on earth did he think he was doing?

Agitated, the second the green arrow lit, Alyx hit the gas pedal. Okay, she told herself as emotions turned her insides into a cruller, calm down; there were another few turns on this road. He would go down one of those. Surely he wasn't trying to find out where she was staying after she'd made it clear she had no interest in picking up where they'd left off?

But parallel to the airport turnoff, she pulled over to the side of the road—and Jonas pulled in right behind her. "Of course," she seethed, "because we both know you aren't headed *there*. You said yourself that you hate to fly!" And he sure wasn't going to buy onto one of those tourist sight-seeing trips in a First World War biplane that soared over the skyline day in and day out, circling the hot-air balloons and gorgeous rock formations.

Having had enough, Alyx thrust open the door. It cost her, but gritting her teeth against the pain in her shoulder, she stood tall and strode back to his purring sports car.

Behind his sunglasses, Jonas's face remained impassive, and he didn't indicate for a second that he intended to get out of the car. "What's the problem now?" he asked.

"You tell me."

Looking off into space, he released the steering wheel to give the palms-up, I-don't-get-it gesture.

"Why are you following me?" she enunciated, hating him for making her spell it out.

"I'm not."

"This is taking things too far, Jonas. Please go away. I don't want to have to notify the police."

Drawing his sunglasses down his nose, he stared at her, a steely glint flashing in his narrowed eyes. "Get over yourself, Alyx. I'm going to work."

"What?" She followed his nod toward the airport. "This is a joke, right? The airport? You happen to have told me that you hate to fly."

"I hate going commercial. I have a private pilot's license, and—sorry to burst your conspiracy theory—I'm helping a friend with his tour service while his broken leg heals."

"I see. Then I apologize for…I apologize." Wishing she could start this day over, or better yet, evaporate into thin air, Alyx returned to Parke's Toyota. Once again her stomach threatened to add to her humiliation and, glancing in the rearview mirror to assure herself that the way was clear, she hit the accelerator and tore away without a last glance at Jonas.

Had to get your drop of blood, didn't you?

Jonas sat still until the black SUV vanished from sight. It bothered him that he hadn't hesitated to embarrass Alyx, but it bothered him more how much he wanted to follow her, to find out if she was telling the truth about the cousin and where the house was. And he'd thought he'd conquered that weakness. When she'd shut him out earlier this year, he'd had his regrets. He could also admit his ego had been bruised, but shortly after arriving back in Washington, D.C., he'd convinced himself that he'd been lucky because then the grandfather of garbage trucks hit the fan, and his personal life got knocked into a different time zone.

Now, with all kinds of opportunity to rethink matters, it was ironic that she should show up. However, he couldn't let that be a trip-switch to acting like a drooling college kid again. His professional clock was ticking and he needed a clear head to make some decisions before the alarm triggered.

As his gaze dropped to his watch, Jonas snapped out of his brooding. He was already minutes late for his first appointment of the day and suspected Zane's phone was seconds away from ringing back at the house as panicking receptionist Miranda attempted to save herself from taking a waiting customer's flack. However, as he continued through the airport entrance, Alyx's face reappeared before him.

He shouldn't have said she looked bad. It would take a mud bath to hide Alyx Carmel's captivating features, and such an event would certainly accent her other outstanding assets, namely her luscious figure.

"Down, boy," he muttered under his breath.

Under no circumstances could he afford to reawaken his libido; he'd mandated a starvation diet for it. The rule was simple: no paycheck, no playtime. Not that Alyx would consider going out with him again.

"'What's done is done.'"

Quoting her, his words sounded more like a puzzle than a vow. But as he pulled up to the Sedona Sites ticket office, he couldn't ignore a tightening in his abdomen that had nothing to do with any concern about Zane's beloved aircraft's air-worthiness and had everything to do with another truth.

Alyx was too close for comfort even for someone with his discipline and willpower.

Chapter Two

As soon as Alyx entered Parke's hillside house, her cousin's greyhound, Grace, drew herself erect from the tile floor in the center of the entryway and stared at her with mournful eyes.

Alyx stopped for a moment to eye the sad creature, as gorgeous a living sculpture as those her owner produced from rock, metal and clay. "C'mon, Gracie, I was as fast as I could be. You have no idea what I went through this morning."

Grace—a racing dog adopted to save her from euthanasia—looked away as though Alyx had insulted her intelligence.

"Okay, your majesty, I know your ancestors wouldn't even let me touch them unless I had a title, and I'm sorry that my absence left you worried about being abandoned again—not that you'll admit it to lowly me. But if you'll give me a moment to pour myself a glass of chardonnay, I'll soak your teeth-cleaning bone in a ladle of your mom's chicken stew. How about that?"

Not waiting for an answer, Alyx eased off her sunglasses and visor and set them and her purse onto the hallway table on her way to the kitchen. Depositing her two bags from the grocery on a counter, she returned to the door of the garage to toe off her sneakers, massaging her shoulder along the way. She felt worse than when she'd entered the fitness center, but right now she had commitments to deal with.

As promised, she got out the pot of chicken stew that was for Grace's dinner and dropped the chew bone in there for a minute while pouring herself the cold wine from a bottle in the refrigerator. After a sip, she sighed and offered the dog the bone.

"There you go. Now behave and don't start wailing and otherwise telling me about your rough morning. Mine was worse and I need to make a couple of calls without sound effects."

Wiping her wet hand on a damp paper towel, she took another soothing taste of the wine. Then Alyx flipped open her cell phone and located E. D. Martel's number in the directory. Martel-Justiss now, she thought with a fatalistic sigh. Her client-turned-dear-friend had not only married Judge Dylan Justiss, but had recently given birth to a third child, Dylan's first, and his namesake. Alyx felt like an amoeba compared to that woman and her courage.

At the sound of E.D.'s voice, she drawled, "How's the mother of the judiciary's next sage?"

"Hey—I've been wanting to call you, but have tried to respect your space. How's it going?" Eva Danielle's tone reverberated with genuine delight. "I expected you to live up to your warning that you'd be out of touch and resigned myself to weeks of worry."

That was one of the many things that made her want to keep E.D. in her life. She might not be comfortable with Alyx's decisions, but she did her best to honor them. "I appreciate that," she told her. "And I'd intended to stay incommunicado, but you know life—make a plan and watch it get a slap shot into the stratosphere."

"Interesting image. You aren't dating a hockey player, are you?"

"Very funny," Alyx replied. "You know I'm not in any shape even to think of such a thing."

"You're a stunner, Alyx. You were before and you still are. My heart aches for what happened to you, and for your suffering. Just know I want to help in any way I can."

Well, then, Alyx thought, here was the perfect opening. She challenged, "Are you aware that Jonas is here?"

"*What?* Of course not! Good grief—how did that happen? You mean *there* there? Sedona?"

"Our paths crossed and I have no idea how that happened." Alyx filled her in on their stressful and unexpected meeting. "I'm sorry to confess that at first I thought maybe you and your deceptively sweet husband had something to do with this," she said at the conclusion of her recount.

E.D. didn't waste a second making a few points. "Did you not threaten to leave without telling me a word for fear of that concern? Why then would I break my word to you?"

"Because you have a soft spot for him and he's one of your husband's most trusted friends."

"All true to a point. However, there are boundaries and

exceptions to things like that and you know it. Neither of us believes in unconditional love, and a confidence is a confidence." E.D. uttered a groan. "I'm sorry you were caught off guard, Alyx, but unless you told someone else, this has to be one of those inexplicable mysteries."

"Destiny? You know my opinion of that."

"Yes, but your perspective is especially vulnerable to emotional influences right now," E.D. said, her tone soothing. "You're still recovering from trauma."

It amazed Alyx that her litigator friend had ever won any case; she was a softy through and through. Smiling despite herself, she asked, "How's Judge Junior?"

E.D. chuckled. "He's like his daddy, too good to be true."

"The next sound you hear may be me snoring."

"Oh, Alyx. I do wish you'd put some body butter on that thick hide of yours and let yourself see what miracles are out there."

"Try to resist suggesting that I adopt, let alone get pregnant."

"I can't deny I've thought about how good that would be for you."

Alyx glanced over at Grace and rolled her eyes. "Lose my phone number. Now!"

E.D. chuckled. "Who else are you going to call to snoop for you?"

She knew that was a joke, but as usual her mind went into overdrive and she immediately thought of P.I.s' phone numbers, only to reject the idea. Jonas would spot the guy in minutes. None of that would happen—crazy she wasn't, even if she was tempted—but it reminded her of how, as a child, she'd been constantly rebuked for "living too much in her head," as her teachers and mother had put it. For once she had to agree with them.

"How are the older kids?" she asked, again hoping to veer their conversation away from her.

"Well, as I hold my breath, Dani is pulling a four-point-zero average at college, Mac hasn't suffered a bad asthma attack in a couple of months, and the baby screams with delight the moment either of them walk through the door. They can't help but drop that entire humiliated-teen act pretending Dylan and I are too old for more children."

"Be careful or one of the TV networks will be courting you to be the next big thing—*un*reality."

"I only shared because you asked."

The gentle rebuke was nothing less than Alyx deserved. "Sorry. I really am happy for you." More like relieved that Dani had straightened out and ceased her declared war on her mother and Dylan. Alyx couldn't imagine herself in such a relationship minefield again, loving as her friend's seemed to have become. "You know my dilemma. My work only shows me the failures in relationships—manufactured or medical—so what you're describing sounds like fiction on the cable channels or the Internet dating sites."

"A few years ago, I would have high-fived you on that. You just keep getting well."

"I want to." Her wording surprised her. Until a few days ago, she couldn't even swear to that. "Um...then you haven't had contact with Jonas?"

"Absolutely not. In fact, come to think of it...he hadn't answered Dylan's last few calls or e-mails."

"He's pretty cryptic about why he's here, too. He says

it's to help a friend who runs a sky-tour business. I had no idea that he was a pilot."

"That makes two of us."

Could that be? Alyx thought, frowning. "But I thought for sure—"

"Until my situation, I didn't know anyone in Dylan's circle."

Alyx barely won over the impulse to take another sip of her wine. She'd believed the two men so close and had suspected this incident was common knowledge by now between husband and wife. On the other hand, she appreciated that she could count on E.D. to keep confidences, as Dylan obviously did.

"There you go thinking again," E.D. said, breaking into her thoughts.

"I'm sorry. I'm nowhere close to my best form and this has…well, it's thrown me."

"Understandable. Now quit beating around the bush and talk to me."

Alyx didn't think she had a choice—she had to get feedback from someone—and gave E.D. a summary of her experiences so far. "Now tell me that I'm overreacting," she said at the end.

"For good reason, considering what you've endured. No one, particularly Jonas, can fault you for feeling anything else but terror at that fool's flagrant advances or for being gun-shy at seeing someone you believed should be on the other side of the continent."

"Yes, but afterward I pushed Jonas away. That's one person I should have trusted—forget the personal stuff." Groaning as her mind churned with hindsight regret, she massaged her aching neck. "It's just that he appeared out of nowhere. Why would he be in the grocery store if he was due at work?"

"Well, my guess is that he saw you on the road—or thought he did—followed you into the market, realized it *was* you, and was trying to figure out why and what he felt about that. Then the incident occurred and the decision was a moot point."

"More stuff that happens in contrived sitcoms, not in real life."

"Tell that to the woman in Belgium who was putting away leftovers for a gentleman friend and found the bodies of his supposedly estranged wife and her son in his cellar freezer."

"What?" Grimacing, Alyx saw that Grace was tilting her head at the door. Alyx quickly crossed to it, tested the lock, and peered through the security hole. "Don't add to my imagination, please. It's in overdrive as it is."

"Sorry. Tell me what else he said. He had to have asked questions. Dylan said he was pretty crushed when you sent him away, and I can't imagine the shock this was for you to see him in a place where you expect to know only your cousin."

Yes, a shock, but also a relief because he had rescued her, Alyx thought with growing guilt. "He wanted an explanation as to why I shut him out. I never gave him one. Did he tell Dylan that?"

"Dylan shared that he sounded frustrated, even hurt a few times, but aside from that, I don't know. He may have committed Dylan to a promise of secrecy, too. You know I won't challenge that without good cause. I feel Dylan would have shared with me if he could."

That said a good deal about his character. Again. As for her own track record with men, Alyx didn't think there was the equivalent of an honorable Dylan among them—unless Jonas could be the exception to the rule? That was probably wishful thinking on her part. Her father had been a dictator, just a grade above bully, and her relationships with men had given her a master's degree in understanding that her primary attraction for most beaus courting her as she grew up were her money, pedigree and contacts. While Jonas hadn't seemed a cookie-cutter replica, their time together had been too short to notice if there was any lasting *there* there.

"You're being ultraquiet," E.D. said.

"I'm remembering moments with Jonas."

"Do you need me to call 911 for a tow to get your mind out of the gutter?" E.D. asked, a smile creeping into her voice.

"Those days are over."

"Alyx, don't talk like that. You're way too young to let even this nightmare deny you the kind of relationship and love I believe is out there for you."

Wanting the comfort of her privacy, Alyx turned professionally cool. "You'll forget I called?"

E.D. made a soft sound of regret. "I really am glad you did. Please. Ring me again. I'm sorry I was of no help, but I am trying…and wanting you to heal."

Hesitating, Alyx stared back at Grace, who'd abandoned the front door to stand before her. No doubt she found her tone discomforting, or wanted her mistress, or would like the front door open to just escape. "You were more help than you know," she told E.D., managing to sound almost tender. "I'm sorry for being such a—anyway, give that luscious baby a kiss for me."

"How sweet. I'll give him two. Call me anytime."

Once Alyx heard E.D. disconnect, she shut off her phone, immediately diving into introspection. Contrary to what she'd said, she hadn't really learned anything she didn't already know, and she'd been trained by the best to be skeptical of support or flattery.

You learned that she and Dylan thought Jonas had been sincerely disappointed in being rejected.

It was hopeless—and perfect. Confirmation that she *was* a hard-hearted, cold witch. *Hurrah,* she thought grimly. She hadn't lost her edge one iota, bad news for the Realtor who wanted to sell her Austin house, but terrific for her Texas clients, who wanted blood from estranged spouses; they, at least, would be popping corks when they heard that reassuring news.

Seeing Grace shift on her plainly stiff legs, Alyx put a quick end to the self-deprecation. "Gracie, if I look half that bad when I wrangle myself off the machines at the health club, you have permission to bite me if I accidentally bump into you or stroke you too hard. Now what do you say we get your stiff-joint medicine? That's about all I know for wrecks like us, until your mommy checks in to suggest something more."

At the sound of *Mommy* Grace started whining.

"Oh, jeez." Alyx leaned over to gently stroke the dog. "I'm sorry, Grace. I'm sorry. I know I'm no replacement by a long shot, but I'm trying—I'll *try* to do better, okay?"

The greyhound stepped closer to rest against her and sighed.

It was too ridiculous to be believable, but Alyx closed her eyes. History had shown her that there were few perfect moments in life, yet this sure felt like one of them. Hoping she could mimic that heartfelt sound, Alyx sighed, too.

Chapter Three

Jonas repressed a surge of humiliation as he dialed Dylan Justiss's private cell phone number, but he managed to hold on until he heard his old friend's rebuke.

"About time."

"Figured you'd deleted me from your address book by now," Jonas replied with equal aplomb. His, however, was mostly bravado.

"You know better than that."

"Yeah, sure. Listen, I'm sorry for the unanswered calls."

"What *ignored* calls?"

That had Jonas's mouth corners curling downward. He knew that Dylan was both letting him off the hook and making sure Jonas understood that he'd slipped badly with their friendship. At the time, he'd felt there was no recourse, and yet, as days slipped into weeks, and weeks into months, he knew he deserved whatever Dylan wanted to say.

"I'm sure there's an appropriate quote about pride to mouth right now, but I can't remember it, and you don't deserve to suffer through it."

"Stuff the eloquence, Hunter. You were never good at it."

That won a choked laugh from Jonas. "That might finally be sinking in. Thanks for sticking in there."

"Well, you know how we analytical types are, I needed to know the answer to the riddle. What happened and how are you?"

"You haven't talked to E.D. this afternoon?" Jonas countered.

"Should I have?"

"I thought maybe…never mind."

"Don't start that. What's up?"

Jonas drew a deep breath. He was sure Alyx had run straight home and had called E.D. to vent. Didn't all women do that? His ex sure had. Claudia would call her mother and then everyone else in the family tree down to second cousins—another reason to avoid getting involved with southern belles. For their part, Alyx and E.D. had grown particularly close during E.D.'s divorce, and Alyx had said that while the svelte, blond DA had a disgusting weakness for Dylan, she was one of the few people she could trust with a secret. He'd still had his doubts.

"I ran into Alyx," he muttered.

"Is that so? Alyx is out of town, maybe out of state from what I can discern from E.D.'s cryptic comments."

"Sedona, Arizona, to be exact."

"Has the divorce rate suddenly skyrocketed there?"

He had to know that she wasn't yet able to resume her usual work schedule. "I don't know what's going on, all I know is that it's just too suspicious to have both of us decide to take leave from our jobs in separate parts of the country and end up in the same place."

"What's your reason?"

"My original flight instructor busted his leg. These days he runs an air-tours business and asked if I could cover for him for a few weeks. He's ex-FBI, too. Back in my mustang days, his was, more or less, the last push I needed to go with the Bureau."

"Good grief, are you saying he crashed and you're now in those hot-air contraptions?"

"Much better. I'm flying his First World War facsimile biplanes."

Dylan uttered something indistinguishable. "You're worse than certifiable. I hope you at least know that?"

"They're the modern Waco rendition. It's a little eccentric, I'll admit, but not as bad as you think. No acrobatics involved, just smooth, wide turns and gentle landings. Everything to assist adventurous tourists in procuring the optimum photographs to bring them back for another visit."

"The question is, can you bring yourself back to earth in one piece? I know a little about the terrain over there. It could get pretty wild trying to find a suitable landing spot on short notice."

The topography *was* a challenge; nevertheless, the highways were excellent and certainly not as heavy with traffic as in metropolitan areas. This was an experience Jonas was glad not to have missed out on.

"And you can take that much time from the job?"

"I have plenty of time built up," Jonas replied evasively. "Look, are you sure E.D. didn't say something about Alyx?"

"Nothing beyond the concern about her, about both of you." After a few seconds Dylan added, "You don't sound like yourself."

"I guess I'm still somewhat—I'm getting too old to play games."

"She wasn't playing games with you," Dylan ground out. "Good God, what's the correct way to behave after coming upon a butchering and almost dying yourself?"

Jonas had gone through all of this dialogue already, had witnessed her being wheeled out to the ambulance and had tried to be supportive and patient, giving Alyx all the time she needed to recover physically and get her balance psychologically. They'd been in the early days of a hot and heavy affair when they'd been thrown into that meat chopper of a bad situation. Regardless of all his attempts to be there for her, even when necessity had demanded he return to Washington, D.C., she'd been the one to sever ties, not him.

"I don't know," he admitted. "But better than what she did."

"What's really got you all bent out of shape now?" Dylan asked. "Get a bad MRI or CAT-scan report after an assignment?"

"Not quite like that. But I guess I'm still trying to find grace under pressure while I work out what's increasingly an uncertain professional future." No one liked to share bad news and this wasn't the moment to elaborate on his. Who knew—right now it was looking like a relief that things weren't going to turn out as he'd first hoped. "I'll let you know the details when I get back to D.C."

"I've still got several minutes before my next appointment."

"I appreciate that, but…"

After another uncomfortable silence, Dylan said, "Whatever you want to do. Jonas, listen…I'm sorry that I came down a little hard on you—"

"You didn't."

"Well, from the little E.D. shared, Alyx deserves support and protection. That's where I was coming from."

"Fair enough."

"Don't hesitate to call. I mean it. And take care."

"I will. And I'll be in touch."

"I'll hold you to that."

Jonas knew Dylan would keep his word and want an update soon. That did nothing to improve his mood for the rest of the evening. Jonas had survived a divorce, managed to keep a decent relationship with his now fifteen-year-old son, and had been holding his breath for an anticipated promotion. When Alyx Carmel had entered his world like a tsunami, he'd been blindsided. He'd never been attracted to female renditions of himself—professional and driven. In fact, he'd avoided dating anyone inside the Bureau or even within coagencies. Yet five minutes after he'd entered her office last year to support Dylan and E.D. during E.D.'s rough divorce, Alyx had him under a spell he had yet to break free of.

He couldn't sleep without being pulled into some intoxicating dream about her. Last night's had been a fuse-buster, a reminder of their first night together.

* * *

"Why did you agree to join me for dinner?" Jonas asked as they sat across a candlelit table from one another. "You know I'm only here for a brief stay."

"You offered me a drink," Alyx replied. "The invitation to dinner was mine."

So it was—a thank-you for helping Dylan help E.D. It struck Jonas, as he'd eyed the steak and lobster plate a waiter suddenly placed before him, that he was tangled in his own web. He'd come after Alyx unabashedly only to find himself snared, and yet the time between ordering and drinking a half glass of shiraz had been one of the most provocative yet awkward times he'd spent with a date. He would ask her a question about herself and if she answered, it was with a single word, "yes" or "no," then asked nothing in return. He'd never felt so inept. Every clever word, his gift for disarming and charming, was a total flop.

It was those smoky gray eyes; they reduced him to ash pudding one minute, then invited a lava-hot heat wave without so much as a blink in the next. He felt as though he was trying to gauge traffic in thick fog. No, it was her scent; he'd fought intoxication for the better part of two hours and had yet to identify it, although he held the office record for guessing what female staffers and agents were wearing. Leave it to this unique woman to refuse to share someone else's creation.

"Okay, seriously," he said at last. "Why did you invite me?"

"Perhaps for the same reason you invited me."

He had to put down his glass. Could she possibly mean it? He'd been fantasizing about a couple of hours of no-strings-attached sex. Someone as cool, confident and pro-

fessional as her couldn't possibly—then, for a second, he saw the diamond-bright shimmer of amusement in her eyes before she lowered a romantic sweep of velvety lashes with the elegant shyness of a geisha.

At the risk of knocking over her glass, he reached across the table to gently lift her chin to search her eyes.

"Why the surprise?" she murmured with a slight arch of one eyebrow. "Wait—don't tell me. You're one of those males who beat a hasty retreat the second you sense conquest?"

For all of his admitted experimental youth, Jonas hoped he'd never been that much of a jerk. "It's been a struggle, but I've almost managed to evolve a step above the penned farm animal."

"Then eat up, Agent Hunter. We can't have you losing your strength."

Things grew decidedly more amiable after that and, in the end, the night was unforgettable. She drove him to her stunning brick home and immediately asked him if she should open another bottle of wine.

"Would you care for any?" he countered.

"Maybe later."

"Exactly my thought."

He took that response as a welcome and initiated a kiss; within seconds Alyx took it—and him—to a different realm. Almost immediately he sensed that he was in deeper waters than he'd expected or intended, but her touch, her taste made her too much of a temptation to resist. When she led him to her bedroom, there was no question about not following. She turned her back to him and murmured, "Unzip me?"

He first touched a kiss to the side of her neck. "I think you're my fantasy come true," he murmured.

"You're off the clock, G-man. Stop thinking so much."
Surrendering, he'd done just that, dropped back onto her
bed and let her take him to a place he'd never been before.

Chapter Four

It took Alyx a few days and considerable humility to accept that therapist Sharleigh had been right to rebuke her for her stubborn lack of cooperation. She had to credit the scene with Jonas for the turnaround, too. How humiliating to have him see her a half year later, still carrying ten pounds she didn't need—especially when she'd been eight under her usual weight when she'd been discharged from the hospital—and moving with the stiffness of someone a decade older.

"Okay, Grace," she told Parke's greyhound on the following Monday. "It's time to swallow my pride and ask Attila the Hunette over at the rehab place to give me another chance. I'll be back in two hours...sooner if she refuses to hear what I have to say, which is entirely possible if your response to me is any guide to go by. But whatever, I'll be back in plenty of time for us to talk to your mommy. Deal?"

The dog just sat like the Sphinx.

"I'll bet you speak your mind the minute you're alone," she told her.

Wondering if she was going to last the full duration of Parke's trip, Alyx climbed into her cousin's Toyota. Talking to the dog as though she was human; what was next? Thank goodness E.D. couldn't see this or she'd never live it down. E.D. had taken to the dog at Dylan's ranch like an extension to her family. Alyx just hoped Grace's wailing stopped before the neighbors notified the police.

Once at the spa, she hesitated; going inside was triggering another wave of dread about what she intended to do. Sucking up had never been an option for her, not when she was a self-doubting law student, nor when she'd walked out of an envied position at a prestigious law firm after deciding making partner wasn't worth sleeping with the man who could vote her in.

By the time she entered the center, her clothes were clinging to her as though she'd already done a thirty-minute workout. But apparently, Shar had been doing some thinking, too, and was grateful to have one less client-patient loss to explain even if Alyx was only a guest. Her lips formed a perfect O when she spotted her, and she actually left another person to greet her.

"Alyx. You're back."

"Don't call security. I'm here to apologize for last week's behavior as soon as I get the glue off the roof of my mouth."

The blond trainer's cheeks bloomed with a delicate peach blush and she began to pant softly with relief. "It's okay. I should never have pushed you as hard as I did. I let myself get caught up in progress and lost sight of the individual."

"I appreciate that." Moistening her lips, Alyx asked, "Is there any room in your schedule to fit me in? I really want to—" she thought of Jonas's grim inspection of her and just as quickly rejected the appeal of seeing desire in his eyes again "—to be able to get out of Parke's hair when she returns. She will need to get back to creating her art, and I have cases coming up in court."

"If you have the time, we can do thirty minutes right now to start getting your body prepared for the real workouts. I'll also show you some yoga stretches to do at home. Then, if you can come tomorrow, I've got an hour open at one."

"I'll take it."

At the end of the half hour, Alyx couldn't pretend that she was any happier than when she'd arrived; in fact, several times she'd needed to blink away tears as Shar worked her through the warm-ups, and even started her on two machines. But the instant Alyx spoke up to point out that she'd reached her limit, Sharleigh assured her that they were through and assisted her off the machine.

"You were great," the therapist said, making notes on her clipboard. "So are we good for tomorrow?"

"Yes, thank you. And I'll make sure to limber up before-hand."

"Super. How's Parke enjoying Italy?"

"She's missing her dog, but she's soaking up a ton of culture and ambiance."

"I envy her the trip. The farthest east that I've gotten so far is Dallas for a conference."

While hardly in a chatty mood, Alyx appreciated the

younger woman's attempt at friendliness. "Well, I haven't done much better than that. What worries me is that she'll have such a great time, she'll stay, and I'll get stuck with her dog."

"You could find a worse place to end up in than here."

Afraid to be taken the wrong way again, Alyx quickly amended, "Oh, Sedona's gorgeous, there's no doubt about it, but I'm just as inexperienced with animals as I am with kids. Definitely not mommy material."

The leggy blonde offered a wry chuckle. "I know a dozen men who would ask for your phone number in a heartbeat. Me, I'd love a half-dozen kids, but once a guy hears that, he loses my number, since most of the singles I meet here have already been divorced at least once and are struggling with child support and facing a future of mountainous college loans."

Alyx couldn't believe this gorgeous blonde had any problem with dating. "I'd think they'd lie until their tongues fell off to get some of your time."

"Ha—yeah, well, the problem is what they want during that time."

Alyx felt ashamed. She knew Shar attracted oodles of attention, but had unkindly assumed the woman enjoyed any and all of it. "I'm sorry about that." Reaching out her hand, she said, "Thank you again for your help and understanding."

Shar smiled and shook her hand. "I'm looking forward to seeing you tomorrow."

Lesson learned, Alyx mused as she left the building. She was ready for a shower for all of the worry, then exertion, as well as something medicinal to rub on her sore muscles and joints, but she was walking with more lightness in her step. This meeting had gone better than expected, and the door was open to continue that progress. She was content.

By the following Monday, Alyx was able to get legitimate praise from Sharleigh and not have to drag herself home only to crash on a couch for an hour or two before being capable of dealing with Grace or any chore. To reward herself, she took a convoluted route home to explore more of the area and picked up fresh dog biscuits at a pet store for Grace, then a thin, organic vegetable minipizza for herself.

She was turning into the airport road when she saw a red biplane take off. Her gut told her it was Jonas, and with her heart thudding, she pulled over and watched the rendition of the vintage craft climb and glisten in the midday sun. There was definitely a person in each seat, which meant he was giving someone a tour. Jonas obviously enjoyed risking life and limb to pilot over such a challenging terrain. Her palms were growing damp at the mere thought of being up there, and she felt a spasm of regret that she'd been so cool and unapproachable last week after the market incident. It wasn't likely that he would be so easy to forgive her as Shar had been. Then again, what if something happened to him during one of those flights and she never let him know she never meant to be unkind?

Giving into another impulse, she turned into the airport and drove up to the air-tours building. Parking beside the other three vehicles there, she leaned over to glance into the rearview mirror. The temptation was fierce, but she wasn't about to primp when anyone inside could see her through the windows and glass door; besides, she was wearing an oversize T-shirt and capri pants—hardly anything to turn heads. She settled for adjusting her white sun visor and brushing away a smear of mascara from under her right eye. What mattered, she reminded herself, was why she was here and what she intended to say.

A little slow getting to the bottom line, Carmel, but at least you made it.

Before she lost her nerve, she went inside. The tan building was modest, a metal corrugated structure; the interior was equally industrial and without much insulation, making Alyx suspect that if you talked loud enough you could hear your voice echoing back to you. How successful this operation was, she had no idea, but the owner didn't waste money on decor.

"May I help you?" a young woman asked from behind the reception counter across the room.

Barely out of her teens, the petite brunette looked Alyx up and down as Alyx crossed the room, and Alyx could have sworn she saw the girl's hazel eyes turn green before they narrowed. Great, she thought, her sixth sense about her sex kicking in; Jonas could have that effect on women just by being polite; there was no telling how sweet Jonas had been to this little cutie with her snug T-shirt bearing the much advertised red biplane stretched across her small breasts and the slogan, I Flew…You Can, Too!

"Oh boy, this is bound to be fun," Alyx murmured to herself.

"Excuse me?"

With a polite smile, Alyx waited until she reached the counter to say, "Hi. I'm looking for Jonas Hunter. I believe he's subbing for the owner here. Was that him in the plane that just took off?" she added, pointing toward the west windows on her right.

"It's not our policy to give out personal information."

Alyx had to compress her lips to keep from enlightening the wren-of-a-girl that she wasn't asking for measurements or financial data. While she knew almost nothing about what made Jonas Hunter tick, she knew more *personal* information about him to keep this little girl blushing through sunset. She also knew from advertisements how long these tours lasted.

"Is this a full-hour flight or a shorter one?"

"That's the customer's business."

"True, but what if I wanted to book the next flight?"

"We take all major credit cards." The girl held out her hand.

Point for Little Miss Sentry, Alyx thought. Seeing that she would just make things worse if she asserted herself, she gave the girl another benign smile and took a step back. "I think I'll wait and get specifics from Mr. Hunter."

"Whatever."

As the girl spun her chair away to return her attention to the computer she'd been working on, Alyx casually walked around the room, pretending an interest in the panel of vacation brochures on the entry wall, no doubt supplied by the local chamber of commerce. There were a few well-worn chairs separated by a vinyl cactus bush and three concession machines offering snacks and soft drinks. A cappuccino dispenser and a free coffee machine were by the restrooms. She suspected a door marked Employees Only led to the hangar. The only hint of a gift shop was the T-shirts piled at one end of the receptionist's counter. Alyx didn't bother checking if they all matched what the receptionist was wearing. She might have bought one to help business by wearing it to the spa, but she didn't have enough cash on her, and she didn't want the teenage watchdog to have any more information about her than necessary.

Jonas must really be helping a *good* friend to be taking off from his demanding work to serve time here.

After pretending to browse through a few pamphlets and eavesdropping on a couple of phone calls, she left the building and returned to Parke's SUV. Keying the ignition and turning on the air conditioner, she backed from the parking lot, then—when away from the window—eased around the building to the back. She saw only one vehicle there—the one Jonas had been driving the other day.

Where was the mechanic, the rest of the staff? Who serviced the planes? If that was Jonas's responsibility, too, there was yet another skill of his that she hadn't known about.

She was frowning as she spotted the plane coming in for a landing. One of the shorter tours after all, she thought...unless there was some kind of mechanical problem?

Adjusting the car's gear to Park, she shut down the engine and got out to watch the plane land smoothly and taxi toward the hangar. Jonas stopped the metal bird about thirty feet away, next to a second, black biplane and shut down its engine. He hoisted himself out before assisting a tall elderly man off the wing and to the ground. After shaking hands, they hugged.

"Great ride, son. Thank you."

"Was it anything like you think your grandfather flew?"

"One difference for sure—no one was shooting at us. Guess you would have to charge extra for that experience."

"And find another pilot." Jonas bowed his head. "He must have been a remarkable man. I'm glad he lived to share the stories with your dad. It was a privilege to take you up. Safe drive on the way back to the hotel. Those pink Jeeps are everywhere at this time of the day. Good enough drivers, but the girls are awfully pretty and apt to turn your head."

Laughing, the man wheezed, "They are that."

As the man left, Jonas turned to her with a surety that told her he'd been aware of her standing there all along. She couldn't tell anything by his expression. He'd slipped off his goggles as soon as he'd cut the engine, and replaced them with his sunglasses. He looked good, though, with his hair whipped by the wind, his face wind- and sun-bronzed, and his black polo shirt and jeans framing a lean and toned body. If he told her to scram without hearing her, she wouldn't blame him, but she would be sorry. So sorry.

"Please don't look at me as though you're afraid that I may be about to announce a pregnancy," Alyx told him, trying for dry humor. "We both know you have nothing to worry about."

"I might not mind if it got you to talk to me."

Was he insane? "I'm about to turn forty, Jonas. By the time a child of mine would be ready for college, the cost will be so high, Donald Trump will need scholarship help."

"From what I've heard on the news, plenty of women are just starting their families at forty."

What was he doing? "Bad joke. I didn't come here to talk about children."

With an indifferent shrug, he asked, "So why are you here?"

She knew if she turned and walked away now, he would let her because she'd shown him that as far as she was concerned, everything was on her terms. Somehow she needed to get through this and get some things said.

"I owe you an apology," she blurted. "I was rude the other day."

He stared back at her with that same give-nothing-away face, then after some seconds, he lowered his gaze to the concrete. "You had your reasons."

"Thank you, but I was being a coward." That got his attention, which told her that he'd been doing considerable thinking about that meeting, too. "Can I simply say that the attack did a lot to undermine my recovered self-esteem? Not having been a social butterfly to begin with, at this point I'm maybe a bad shopping trip away from being a recluse."

Jonas abruptly looked away. "That put-down regarding your appearance was—it was crap, Alyx. You could never look bad."

With a wry twist of her lips, Alyx replied, "You are a gentleman."

"No, if I was, I'd never have lashed out like I did. It was a cheap shot." He sighed. "And you still haven't learned to take a compliment." His gaze fell to her shoulder. "You didn't have any other repercussions from that slug who grabbed you last week?"

"No. I'm sure the manager was so humiliated that he threatened his relative's life himself. But I plan to give my cousin a heads-up when she returns. She doesn't need to experience that or worse."

Jonas nodded. "Good idea. How long before she gets back?"

"About three more weeks. How about you?"

"Just about the same if Zane doesn't go crazy on me and launch himself off his ten-foot-high balcony into the dry riverbed making this whole effort moot."

"Another good patient, eh? Your karma must be catching up with you, Hunter."

He bit off a laugh and folded his arms across his chest. "Or something."

Alyx wished he would take off the sunglasses so she could see his silvery-blue eyes. But she supposed she deserved this restriction. She wasn't religious, but she was spiritual and believed in the concept of penance.

"You're able to take that much time off from the Bureau?" His expression gave nothing away, and yet Alyx felt his armor come up as though a medieval castle had suddenly slammed all doors. "Sorry, sorry," she said quickly. "I didn't mean to intrude."

"I'm on leave."

Of course he was. He'd said as much. What had he said? She'd been so caught up in her own misery that it must never have registered for more than seconds. Alyx mentally hit her palm to her forehead.

"I expected a promotion and didn't get it."

Stunned that he would share so much, Alyx wanted to respond with compassion and so was slow to do so. "I'm—"

"Never mind. It doesn't matter."

Recovering, Alyx frowned. "Of course it matters, Jonas. I just have no right to ask about your personal business."

"It was for Chief of the Austin office, that district."

"Austin…?" He'd wanted to move to Austin? Since

when? Did this have anything to do with her? It couldn't possibly; they hadn't known each other long enough for something like that. It must have been to get closer to Dylan and E.D. "I'm so sorry. Do they know?"

"Who?"

"Dylan and E.D."

"No, Alyx," he repeated monotonously. "They don't know and I'd appreciate it if it stays that way."

"Of course." She didn't know how she felt about the news herself. What would it have been like if they hadn't been a half-day's travel apart? "Did they tell you why they didn't give it to you?"

"They don't do that," Jonas said with the calm of someone trained to pass a lie detector test. "They stick to the 'most qualified agent and seniority' jargon. But it was politics and everyone involved knows it. I'm a little less of a 'yes, sir' man and less politically correct than the guy who got the position. My divorce, despite being old news for a couple of years now, didn't help. The man with the final stamp of approval has a thin skin regarding giving up on marriage and a long penchant for resentment for anyone who does, regardless of the reason."

"That's—" Alyx bit her tongue to keep from saying too much. It was her experience that the very people who censured others would be better off keeping their noses in their own business. "Can you fight it?"

He grunted. "Even if I could, would the end results be worth it? It's not smart to be seen as challenging authority if you're hoping to get their support down the road."

"I don't know what else to say except that I hate this for you."

"Thanks."

And to think that when he had been in the most need of support, she had symbolically slammed a door in his face. Under the circumstances, she wouldn't have been any help, but she knew from experience that sometimes listening made all the difference.

"If you're under the perception that I feel you should bear some guilt over this, don't be," Jonas said. "It wasn't to be…none of it."

There was that word again. *Perception* had popped into her head several times in the last few days since being reunited with him. They'd certainly been guilty of being wrong about each other, jumping to conclusions without asking or having all of the facts.

"So what happens now?" She didn't want to hear any more bad news, and why she was prolonging this conversation she couldn't fathom for the life of her, but the sympathy and questions kept spilling through her lips as fast as water through a burst faucet during a winter freeze.

"I'm trying to decide. I guess that's why this situation with Zane was so appealing to me. It could buy me time to think."

Flying two tongue depressors attached to a motor was a sane formula to figuring out the rest of your life? Alyx knew he was vested for his pension—it was easy to do the math since he'd previously informed her that he'd joined the Bureau right after college—but only just. Plus that wasn't the only thing to consider.

"You can't quit the Bureau?" Seeing his eyebrows rise above the sunglasses, she sighed in self-exasperation. "Let me rephrase that. I meant, aren't you worried—considering the age of your son—of expenses coming up? College, for example?" But as soon as the questions had been posed, Alyx touched her fingers to her lips. "Forgive me. It's none of my business."

Jonas shrugged. "No, but I don't mind. At any rate, I'll sort it all out before Blake graduates and spends what I've already put aside for him. It isn't my way to let anyone else carry my load."

Meaning ex-wife Claudia's new and very wealthy husband. No, Jonas was no less proud than she was. They still knew next to nothing about each other's familial history, but it wasn't all about DNA. Character was about nurturing, too, and she was beginning to suspect they had more in common than she initially concluded.

"No, you would never." After those soft words, Alyx smiled an over-bright smile and took a step back. "Well, I've taken up enough of your time. I wish you luck, Jonas. Really. With everything."

"Thank you, Alyx. It was generous of you to do this."

"No, just necessary."

Feeling as though she'd been given her cue that he didn't want to hear any more—and she knew she should have left a minute ago—she remained rooted in place. The reason wasn't a mystery; she was suddenly realizing this was probably the last time she would ever see him.

"Alyx—"

As Jonas took a step closer, Alyx also heard a door squeak open behind her. Then she heard a sweet voice call out.

"Jonas? I'm sorry to bother you, but I have a problem on the phone? I'd call Zane, but he's at the doctor's for a checkup."

"Be right there," he called back to Miranda. To Alyx, he said, "Sorry. I do need to take that. Do you want—"

"I'm late anyway," Alyx interjected quickly and backed toward the SUV. "The dog gets pretty stressed if I'm gone too long. Take care, Jonas. And I mean that."

Before he could get another word out, she was climbing into the vehicle.

Imbecile, she chastised herself as she fumbled to get the key in the ignition. She didn't know the perfect exit line when she heard it. He forgave her, and that's all she'd come for, all she needed. Now they could move forward with a clear conscience and goodwill.

But as she drove away from the airport, Alyx couldn't deny a bittersweet something twisting her heart.

Chapter Five

Mechanical problem...what mechanical problem?

On Wednesday, stopped in the middle of carrying her laundry to the washroom in Parke's house, Alyx gasped at what she thought she'd heard on the radio and raced back to the kitchen to turn up the volume.

"We are just getting in this report that a tour plane—the biplanes so popular in Sedona—looks as though it will be forced to make an emergency landing. Where that's going to happen, we're not exactly sure. Nor are we aware of the reason for the alert, but a representative of the company has told us that there are no passengers on board. That is at least a bit of good news. We will bring you updates as they come available."

Good news to whom? Alyx wondered, her chest tightening. That was Jonas up there, she just knew it! There were two other fly-tour businesses operating at the airport that she knew of, but one was a helicopter service and the other a yellow Cessna type of plane with a closed cabin. Yes, it had to be Jonas in trouble.

Suddenly weak-kneed, Alyx almost dropped onto the leather ottoman by the fireplace. If it weren't for her now-constant shadow, Grace, she probably would have.

The greyhound nudged her as though suspecting Alyx had forgotten the way to the washroom.

"Grace, let's go outside for a minute, and then I have to leave for a few minutes."

It clearly wasn't what the poor girl had in mind, but ten minutes later, Alyx, still dressed in the pastel-green knit top and darker green capri pants that she'd been doing her chores in, grabbed the keys, her wallet, and ran for the garage. There was no question about waiting for the radio to tell her what was happening. Something compelled her to see for herself that Jonas landed safely.

The traffic was congested almost from the moment she left Parke's cul-de-sac, no surprise, considering the alert, but it quickly had Alyx regretting her decision to try to reach the airport when she found herself in the thick of media vans and other gawkers. Everyone wanted to see if a newsworthy crisis was about to occur. As she inched toward the airport, she passed many a person with a video phone aimed at the sky, first cousins to the rubberneckers eager to see the ambulances and bodies after a bad traffic wreck on a highway, then to get their name mentioned on network TV. She had no business adding to that. Jonas certainly wouldn't welcome her presence. But the question kept repeating in her head, what if this did turn into a worst-case scenario?

In the end, Alyx compromised. She parked diagonally in the gap she spotted between two vans only a few yards outside of the airport entryway. Grabbing her keys, she locked her car, leaving her wallet and everything but her sunglasses to follow the chatty stream of the curious and the media toward the landing strip.

She heard the plane's approach almost immediately and spotted it moments later. To her horror, it was sputtering and coughing like an emphysema patient gasping for oxygen and yet another puff on a cigarette.

"Look at that thing," a man to her right said. "At that low speed, he could drop like a bowling ball."

Tightening her fingers around the keys, Alyx pressed her hand to her heart. Couldn't planes glide for a while? Maybe you needed wind? There was no wind to speak of. The realization made her all the more worried for him.

"Come on," she whispered under her breath. She prayed he was in control of his faculties, that he had the skill he claimed to have to land that thing, that he didn't have a moment of thinking, *What the hell difference does it make if I survive?*

As the left wing suddenly dipped, everyone on the ground, including Alyx, gasped, plus she shifted her fist to her lips. From the corner of her eye, she saw a fire engine race toward the landing strip, yet another hint of how dangerous the situation was.

In terrifying slow motion the biplane coughed and wobbled its way to earth with a stream of smoke pouring from it and, as it touched concrete, a screech from braking tires. As soon as it stopped, Jonas pulled himself out of the plane, hopped to the ground, and began running away, apparently concerned himself about a possible explosion.

Breathing a sigh of relief after seeing nothing on his black polo shirt and jeans to suggest he was injured, Alyx took exception to the disappointed sigh from one man.

"Excuse me, a man didn't turn into a fireball, and you're sorry?" she demanded.

He barely gave her a look as he shut off his phone. "I'm behind on my child support. This could have been a windfall to help me catch up."

After weeks of trying to keep her head down, Alyx couldn't help but think of some of her recent cases, the lowlifes that made her fight so hard and long, and risk so much. "I'm an attorney. What's your wife's name so that I can help her put you where you belong?"

The man backed away from her as though she'd just confessed to being contaminated with the latest superbug, then vanished into the retreating crowd. That was all she really wanted. Returning her attention to Jonas, who was now shaking hands with the firefighters, she absorbed the sight of him with relief and a strange pride. She would just watch a moment longer, she told herself, then return to the house. With all of these people around, he would never spot her.

The thought had barely passed through her mind when he looked over someone's shoulder and his eyes locked with hers.

Was that…? Yes, it was Alyx.

Jonas didn't consider himself a romantic. He thought he'd made his share of romantic gestures when inspired, but he certainly had never bought into the love-at-first-sight concept, regardless of Dylan and E.D.'s remarkable history. However, realizing Alyx had come up with this ridiculous crowd to watch his landing, he experienced an unusual jolt and had to struggle to pay attention to police and firefighters. He was beyond grateful to be on the ground intact, and for these good people's quick response, but it frustrated him that he couldn't go ask why she had come. She'd made it clear that they were history, so why bother? Another gesture to prove her sincerity that she wished him well? He sure didn't want her pity if he had crashed. Send a bottle of Scotch to the memorial service, he thought with an increasing touch of sarcasm. Heck, he wanted a double now, but since he expected to test-fly Zane's increasingly temperamental plane as early as tomorrow, that wasn't even an option for him tonight.

"Jonas!" Miranda rushed through the hangar and toward him. Her coral-pink tank top delineated her youthful curves to perfection, as did her jeans, while her glossy chestnut ponytail swung, catching the midday sunlight. He suspected his teenage son would salivate over her, although she was three or four years too old for him. And Jonas was *decades* too old for her, but that didn't stop the kid from trying to throw her arms around him. Seeing her intent in those deceptively kitten innocent eyes, he caught her by her forearms and pretended to steady her.

"Watch it. Don't fall," he said before turning to face the fire chief to make sure she didn't try anything else.

"Are you okay?" she gushed. "I was terrified. I only waited inside just long enough to call Zane to assure him that you were on the ground."

"I'm fine. Thanks for the concern, and for reassuring

Zane. Did you tell him that his plane hasn't suffered any structural damage?" Seeing her worshipping gaze dim, Jonas nodded toward the building. "You'd better go reassure him."

He spoke kindly, not wanting to embarrass her in front of the others. He was pretty certain Zane could turn on the TV and see for himself, considering the TV video cameras trained on them, but it worked to get the kid out of his hair.

It took longer to get rid of the press. The media wanted something for what, in effect, was wasting their time. About twenty minutes later, when Jonas had satisfied the reporters enough to excuse himself, and all of the emergency trucks pulled away, there was no sign of Alyx, either.

Heck, he thought, going inside to call Zane, maybe she'd been a figment of his imagination. Wishful thinking after something of a scare.

Minutes later Zane's grumbling got Jonas's mind back in focus.

"That fuel pump isn't a year old," Zane fussed. "Cost a pretty penny, too. Couldn't be anything else."

"You're welcome for me bringing down the plane in one piece." Jonas couldn't help but smile at the way his friend got straight to his priorities.

"Next time use the parachute. I'm starting to feel like the insurance premium isn't worth the expense of keeping those old girls airborne."

"Parachute? You failed to mention exit accoutrements are included in this deal. As cheap as you are I wouldn't trust it wasn't one of Betty's tablecloths stuffed in that case."

"Oh, you know I'm grateful. Damn it all, I'd never have forgiven myself if something happened to you. Let's just forget this deal. You cancel any reservations on the books—Betty already said that's what we should do—and I'll use this downtime to rethink matters. In fact, I'll be there in less than thirty minutes to post notice myself and write Miranda a check to get her through the month so she can make her next car payment and still look for another job."

"You stay put. You know the doctor said you're supposed to keep your butt home, and your leg up."

"They don't pay my insurance premiums."

"Just stay put anyway. Think this through and if it's what you really want, she can come to your house tomorrow for the check, but don't jump to any life-changing decision because of me. I make my own decisions and choose my own risks."

Jonas sent Miranda home after that but stayed to study the plane for another couple of hours. What else did he have to do? Zane and his wife, Betty, deserved some quiet time to talk—as loudly or passionately as they wanted to—without being aware he was in the guest room.

By the time he locked up and started down the road, he had an idea in his head that was too tempting to pass on. It had arrived just after he'd reported to Zane that he thought he had the plane ready to test again. He'd had Zane call in a favor or two and figured out the rest of Alyx's cousin's name and got her address.

As he entered her road, a hilly and winding dead end, he was captivated by the unique adobe southwestern architecture...until he saw a shapely brunette pretending to chase a leggy hound around an SUV. That couldn't be Alyx, he told himself. She wasn't athletic, and while he knew she was here to watch a dog as part of her responsibility to her cousin, she wasn't a huggy-feely animal lover. But as she rounded the corner of the RAV4 again, he recognized that green outfit she was wearing—and that blond dog was a greyhound all right.

He pulled up to the curb and saw her pause as she stared at the Mustang. The dog stopped like a statue before her and looked from him to her. Sensing it was well-behaved, he climbed out to walk over to them.

"You," she murmured as he stopped maybe two yards away.

"Yes." He glanced down at the sleek greyhound who eyed him with curiosity, if not complete trust. "Is he okay to pet?"

"She. Her name is Grace and she's reserved but loving when she warms to you."

Jonas crouched down, despite some knee pain from bumping his leg during the imperfect landing today. "Well, hello, Grace. You are a child of your ancestors, aren't you? It looks like you've warmed to your babysitter."

"No one is more stunned than me," Alyx admitted, crossing her arms under her breasts.

After Jonas stroked the dog for another minute, he rose and met Alyx's own nervous gaze. It was good to see color in her cheeks even if it was exertion mixed with embarrassment that he'd seen her at play—or at least relaxed.

"How did you find me?"

He pointed overhead. "Friends in high places."

Her gray eyes went wide. "You went up again? In that…*thing?*"

He shrugged. "What goes down has to go up again. But not yet. No, what I meant was that I had friends find your cousin's address."

"The same person or people you're helping?"

"Let's say friends of friends."

"Once an operator always an operator."

"Come on, like you haven't used your resources outside of a trial?"

"No."

"I don't believe you."

"You're calling me a liar?"

The calmly posed question had Jonas backpedaling fast. He'd meant to tease and challenge, not accuse. Since when had she become so sensitive? Just as quickly he wanted to slap his palm against his forehead. No, she would use any resource for a client, but never merely for herself. It would remind her too much of her father's opportunistic ways.

Backtracking, he opened the Mustang's passenger door and picked up the bouquet of flowers on the leather seat. Returning to her, he offered the token he'd detoured to pick up on his way, a robust bouquet of sunflowers and eucalyptus. "I'm not saying that," he continued. "What I meant to do by coming here was to thank you for checking on me."

Alyx focused on the bouquet. At first he worried she might reject them; then she slowly reached out her hands.

"I didn't intend for you to see me."

"I figured that out when I looked again and you'd vanished."

"I wanted to get out of there before your office girl spotted me. She's rather territorial about you."

Jonas rolled his eyes. "The less said about that, the better. I'm hoping if I ignore it, she'll get the hint and aim for someone in her own age bracket."

"Don't hold your breath or you'll end up in Emergency after all."

Looking pained, he asked, "Can we change the subject?"

"I'm glad you're all right."

Much better, he thought, filling his lungs with satisfying air. "It wasn't as scary as it looked."

"Spoken like someone who still has adrenaline racing through his veins." Alyx touched the saffron-yellow petals of the sunflowers. "Thank you for these. How did you know they're my favorite?"

"You had them on your entryway table at your house the first night you invited me for a drink, and there's an oil painting of a bouquet of them above the buffet in your dining room."

"Ever the perceptive G-man. Would you like to come in for something cool to drink?"

"Only if you really mean it and aren't just being polite." He already knew the answer she'd give him. Having cheated death herself, Alyx Carmel no longer did anything she didn't want to do.

"Come in before the nosy neighbors rush out for an introduction. They're a sweet elderly couple with too much time on their hands. I don't know how Parke gets any work done."

She led the way up the curved sidewalk lined by river rock and otherwise adorned by various cacti, some blooming delicate pink, and others looking dangerous enough to impale an ox. The front door was a massive oak creation etched in glass; the iron and glass chandelier Jonas passed under looked heavy and expensive.

"No wonder your cousin has a pharaoh's dog," Jonas said, looking around the foyer. "Her eye for form is exceptional."

"Grace is retired from the racing world and lucky not to have become an entrée in a third-world restaurant," Alyx said, keeping her voice low. "She was bred for track pups, and when few champions emerged, her owners intended to put her down. You wouldn't believe how many of these poor creatures get killed every year when they're no longer of financial value to their owners. Parke joined some rescue group that adopts them."

It was probably his imagination, but from the sadness that suddenly darkened the dog's eyes, Jonas would have sworn she understood every word Alyx said. He stroked the canine's back soothingly. "I hope things are much better now, Gracie." To his delight, the dog raised a paw to "shake." "I guess you are a twenty-four-carat doll," he chuckled and complied.

To Alyx he added, "It was good of your cousin to do that."

Alyx closed the door behind them. "Yes. Very. It surprised me that she did it. Parke and I are alike in that we're not...well, she's obviously achieved a spiritual understanding of nature that I've yet to champion."

"Grace seems to enjoy your company."

She and the dog had enjoyed the little romp from the mailbox to run around the RAV. Alyx hadn't planned it; it was something Grace had instigated. Not knowing what else to say, she gestured toward the interior of the house. "What will it be? Tea or lemonade?"

"How do you know about the rules of a pilot drinking?"

Alyx led the way down a marbled hallway, through an expansive wood-floored living room to an open kitchen. "A former client was a commercial pilot. I just assumed the rules were pretty much standard for anyone in a cockpit."

As the elegant Grace veered to the living room and gingerly climbed onto the leather couch, Jonas followed Alyx, admiring the airy kitchen with the center island. "Whatever you're having will be great."

"Iced tea it is. I should warn you it's peach-flavored."

"Should I be scared?"

Alyx smiled as she filled two glasses with ice from the dispenser on a stainless refrigerator. "Usually, I avoid flavored teas and coffees, but Parke keeps tons of this on hand and I haven't been hospitalized yet."

Jonas was a purist himself as far as liquid consumption was concerned, but was busy taking in his surroundings. "This place is nothing short of spectacular. Your cousin is doing well with her work. Ha!—great mini–wine cooler," he added as he spotted the pint-size refrigerator that on first glance looked like a dishwasher.

"I gave Parke that for her birthday after she'd sent me the bronze cactus-and-coyote pup piece that you liked at my house."

"She did that piece?" Jonas had meant to ask, since it had impressed him immediately. At that time, though, their relationship had been all about seduction and lust. "She's fantastic."

"That's why she's in Italy. She's been taken under the wing of some—" Alyx gestured, at a loss for words "—mentor—who is personally involved in guiding her through the ruins, museums and private collections, opening her eyes anew to the masters and exposing her to *la dolce vita.*"

Jonas tested the phrase on his tongue. "I actually saw some of that movie back when I was a teenager. Don't remember coming upon any nude scenes," he added, pretending all seriousness. "I'm pretty sure I flipped channels hoping that I'd find some—or else a football or basketball game."

Handing him a moisture-beaded glass, a smiling Alyx replied, "I believe that."

Determined to keep things lighthearted—even at the expense of his own reputation—he continued, "So, this guide is an actual teacher-mentor? Not a lover?"

"I haven't asked, and she's not likely to tell."

There was nothing else for Jonas to do but taste the tea. "It's good."

"Perhaps before you leave Arizona, you can sample one of Parke's collection of wines that were created by another acquaintance."

"Got it," he replied, slowly nodding as though indexing data. "Not a friend…but she may have done work for him?"

There were times Alyx's slicing gaze could laser the wings off a gnat, but on this occasion her glance suggested that she enjoyed his lightheartedness.

"She did do work for him. The iron-and-stone entry gate for his vineyard is her creation. A sketch is on every label. Check it out."

She retrieved a bottle from the cooler. Jonas couldn't help but whistle in admiration at the captivating work and could only conclude such creativity was inspired by great wine. "If I grovel adequately, will you let me see her studio?"

"You're a collector of art?"

He could have kissed her there and then. She drove him nuts when she pulled that haughty, under-her-lashes-and-down-her-nose diva look. "You know what I collect," he replied, challenging her gaze with his own. "Criminals. But

I don't want to leave Arizona without seeing all of the reasons why people from both coasts and other countries flock here like brides going to one of those once-a-year gown sales. Have you watched the tour buses unload? There are, of course, the grunge dressers who are only interested in a T-shirt and key chain that will end up in a junk drawer, but I've seen some visitors wait over an hour to photograph sculpture in the best light. As gorgeous as the rock formations are here, there's architecture and sculpture that's been photographed just as much."

What a revelation to hear him share such curiosity and cultural awareness. The few times they'd eaten out together, Alyx had observed that Jonas enjoyed the dining experience, and it wasn't about show or indulging in the expensive; he really had studied menus, enjoyed the tasting and sharing experience. But he also confessed to rarely indulging and admitted he mostly got through demanding schedules and grueling travel by surviving on frozen dinners.

"I've seen a few incidents similar to your tour bus experiences," she told him. "In fact, it was a kick to see someone take family photos in front of one of Parke's downtown sculptures. She is good at what she does."

"So are you."

Alyx knew she was looking at him as though he'd switched languages from English to a lost tongue. Why did he think he needed to reassure her? No, she resented him for breaking the magical moment.

As she began to turn away, Jonas touched her arm. Reluctantly, she glanced back at him.

"Tell me why you wouldn't see me, talk to me after the

attack? I understand how that two-legged pig threw you off your stride, but you're a fourth——or is it fifth-?—generation steel magnolia? The Alyx Carmel I knew would never let a creep like that keep her down."

"Thank you. I think I have scars to prove that I succeeded."

Some might consider that a gut punch, and she would have been the first. As soon as she saw him flinch, she regretted her retaliation. But it was too late.

"Can we sit down?" he murmured. "I think the day's excitement is about to catch up with me."

Alyx immediately beckoned him to one of the iron-and-caramel-suede kitchen barstools. "What can I get you? Should I call 911?"

"Don't even think of it."

"Tell me what to do!"

"Avoid going into nursing." Jonas set the tea glass on the soapstone counter. "I think a glass of that cabernet would be a smarter choice. Please. And don't think about opining about that, either. There won't be any flying tomorrow." Watching her go to work, he continued to make his point. "You know I *have* had sensitivity training—not to mention intravenous doses of diplomacy. All it takes to trigger either is communication."

Handing him his wine, she poured for herself as well. "I'm sorry for going for the jugular."

"And I swear I'm not here for payback or to judge you. Can we drop any further references to our professional work?"

"I don't know. Maybe we've been who we are for too long."

Jonas grunted. "Now that *is* defeatist."

Alyx set to work rocking the kinks out of her neck. "The word is *tired*. Look, my father trained my brother and me to be workaholics and overachievers. No, not just trained—indoctrinated. He was extremely pushy and highly competitive. Our house wasn't a home, it was an Ivy League MBA course with something like a boxing club for recreation, only it wasn't called that, it was called *seasoning*. You get my point?"

"I'm not sure that I do. Your father beat you?"

"He didn't have to, all he had to do was get you into a ring with someone he'd rent for the day…then he would stand on the side and—encourage. His skills with language and disdain alone could turn you into a pugilist. I read or heard somewhere that Cameron Diaz broke her nose, what, three times? Surfing. I've got her beat and never stepped into an ocean until I was thirty.

"Unfortunately, my brother, only a year younger than me, but a gentler soul, couldn't take that kind of pressure. After the one time my father did put on gloves with us, Lone committed suicide."

"Alyx…"

Looking overwhelmed as she'd never seen him, Jonas put down his glass. All she needed to do was meet his gaze and he would have taken her into his arms, but she saw enough out of the corner of her eye to make her stare hard at the speckled soapstone counter and will him to keep his distance.

"*Lone* is a sad name," Jonas said at last.

Alyx nodded in slow motion. "Our father was intuitive in that way. He knew immediately that Lone would be what he saw as weak and would need reminding that one went through life alone and shouldn't look to anyone for help."

"And he named his daughter to be a warrior?"

She only managed half of a smile. "Fooled him, though. After Lone died, I switched my focus from corporate law to family law."

"He undoubtedly railed that there was no money in that."

"Unfortunately, there's plenty, even after all of the *pro bono* cases."

They sat there in a strangely comfortable silence; seconds could only be counted by when either of them took a breath. "I miss the sound of birds. Have you noticed there aren't as many birds here? I miss being wakened by the birds that roost in the bushes outside my bedroom window in Austin. Not enough vegetation or water to sustain them, I guess."

"You were the one to find your brother," Jonas said instead of replying. "No wonder years later you raced to Cassandra Field's house without telling anyone after Dylan's swearing in. You probably didn't think at all. All you wanted to do was defend her from the monster she had called husband as you hadn't been able to defend your brother against your father."

An officer later told her that he'd never seen such a vicious crime scene. Alyx had arrived on the tail end of a perfect storm of violence, and was caught between a man who would not accept failure or rejection and a woman asking only for the dignity of a quiet independent life.

"Alyx…may I?"

Lost deep in her thoughts, Alyx was slow to realize that Jonas had risen from the barstool. He wanted to hold her.

"I didn't tell you that so that you would pity me," she said, frowning at her glass. "If anyone deserves—"

"Stop." Jonas gently turned her chair and eased her to her feet. "It's not pity. I'm just...I'm damned sick of all of it."

Feeling his arms come around her, Alyx realized that she hadn't been this close to a man since the night before the attack. Her body responded accordingly, trembling from long restraint and tension. Even the blood surging through her veins seemed to be a discordant mixture of hot and cold. What to feel...what to feel? it seemed to be asking.

"I'm sorry that first SWAT officer was such a good shot," Jonas said against her hair. "I would have carved that man up with the dullest knife in that house."

Alyx shuddered.

"Am I touching someplace that's still tender?" he asked immediately, gentling his hold.

"No. The worst lingering pain is in my shoulder. I just don't want to think about all that again. It took long enough not to see him whenever I closed my eyes."

Jonas shifted to touch his lips to her left shoulder. Even through the cotton of her blouse, Alyx felt the warmth.

"You want to tell me where else it hurts?" he murmured.

Tempted to brush her fingers across her breast, she made herself step back. "You've been extremely kind, Jonas, but..."

"It's better if I drink the wine...which is marvelous. My compliments to your cousin's friend."

"I'll be sure he gets the message. It probably isn't every day that he gets praise from one of the government's finest."

Jonas cast her a warning look from under his eyebrows. It would have been intimidating but for the dismay in his eyes when he noted the trembling in her hand as she picked up her own glass. She would have blushed with embarrassment but had lost that ability so long ago, she'd forgotten what it felt like.

"Relax," Jonas said, breaking into her thoughts. "I'm going." He polished off the wine and set the goblet with impeccable care onto the counter. "But I'm going to make one request."

"What's that?"

"If you get a wild impulse to stop by the airport, don't fight it."

Alyx swirled the contents of her own glass. "There are times between midnight and three in the morning when I do pace around Parke's studio hoping to get tired enough not to have to fill buckets and mop floors."

Jonas pretended to take her reply seriously. "At that hour the gates are locked and there's a security guard on duty. While I've no doubt he would enjoy your company, I'd prefer you come to talk to *me*."

"Well," she began slowly, "you managed to lure me there twice already despite my being warned off by young Miranda. Who knows what may happen?"

Jonas made a face. "So you noticed that little problem."

"Nineteen is the new thirty—sexually speaking. She's determined that you will notice her."

"I'll keep my guard up."

He got to the living room before he did an about-face and returned to her. Taking hold of the iron back of her stool, he turned her to face him.

"While you're focusing on what everyone else is doing, try to keep this in mind."

Then he locked his mouth to hers in a gentle but without question an I-will-not-be-ignored kiss.

It was over before she could think to pull away, and there was something in his step that made her not only follow him but watch him through the distortions of the glass entryway as he strode to the Mustang. None of that eased her yearning for more.

Chapter Six

"Did I wake you?"

As soon as she awakened to the ringing phone, Alyx knew it was Parke, and as she listened to her question, she sat up in bed and checked the clock. Although it was almost daylight in the room, quick math told her that her cousin had once again forgotten the time difference. It was about the hour that vino began pouring in Italy. But then, to Parke, it was almost always a good time for wine.

"No, I was lying here trying to decide what to do with my day. After a workout at the gym," she added, hoping to avoid a lecture from her cousin. "How are you?"

"Miserable. It's raining…again. I can't get the lighting I need for this landscape that I wish I'd never started, and I was stood up for lunch. Tell me some wonderful news so I don't fall into the black hole of lousy moods."

"Have pity, Parke, I haven't even had my first dose of caffeine yet. In fact, Venus is still peeking around the edge of the miniblinds."

"Is she? Oh, blast, I'm sorry, sweetie. Hang up and go back to sleep."

"Easy for you to say." Throwing back the green satin bed sheet, Alyx shifted to the side of the bed and scratched upside-down Grace's tummy with her toes. "Morning, Gracie. It's your mommy on the phone."

The greyhound immediately wriggled right side up and whimpered.

"Oh, how's my girl? Let me talk to her a second, Alyx."

Grinning at her cousin's sweet but fun entreaty, she replied, "Of course. I knew the real reason you called."

Lowering the handset to the dog's left ear, she asked, "Who's this, Grace?"

She watched the dog's eyes widen as she leaned into the phone, then writhed as Parke baby-talked to her. When Grace yelped and ran from the room, Alyx put the handset back to her ear. "Well done. She'll be glued to the front door waiting for you to get home and when you don't come, she'll refuse to eat and she'll look at me like I'm the bad guy."

Parke sighed. "I'm sorry, but I miss her."

"You need a life."

"If by chance you mean a man, I could say 'Go stand in front of a mirror and say that again.'"

As Jonas's image flashed before her eyes, Alyx pushed herself to her feet and padded down the hall to the kitchen, her white satin nightshirt brushing against her thighs. What she needed was coffee if she was going to have this conversation. "The point I was trying to make is that if you can't find romance in the country of love, what's the point of being there?"

"France, specifically Paris, is the assumed center for love."

About to suggest she book a flight, Alyx's attention backtracked. "What's wrong with your date's eyesight that he stood you up?"

"It wasn't a romantic rendezvous. He's practically sixty, for pity's sake."

"Wow," Alyx drawled. "Almost old enough to be an uncle."

"Keep at it and you can forget the thank-you present I was going to bring you for watching Grace and the house for me."

After her own rough day the day before, she couldn't continue taunting her relative. "You don't have to bring me anything, but I am sorry for teasing you. Is the gentleman in question an artist, too?"

"A dealer. He could have been a welcome conduit in selling my work here."

After switching on the coffeemaker, Alyx swept the heavy fall of her hair back from her face. She knew very little about how Parke's business operated, and except for a few paintings she'd bought at local fairs and the pieces Parke had given her through the years, she avoided the social scene of showings at galleries. "Isn't that what the Internet is for? E-Bay…Craig's List, to name the two I've heard about."

"You know I'm almost computer illiterate, and who has time to do all of that clerical work and whatnot? I'd have to hire someone, which defeats the purpose of having a studio in my home so I don't have to deal with people underfoot. Plus I don't want to be bothered with all of the minutiae of selling and collecting payment. That's the whole point of having a rep who believes in me and knows immediately who to target."

"It sounds complicated, and tedious—and potentially dangerous. How do you know that you won't get ripped off, and who to trust? It takes you so long to create your work."

"There's risk in every business. After what you've been through, surely you can see that?"

"Well, you have me there." Alyx couldn't help but touch her wounded shoulder. "So what do you think happened to the guy? Where did you meet him?"

"At Corrado and Ilsa's dinner party on Sunday."

Alyx recognized the names as those of the couple who were Parke's hosts during her stay in Italy. "Maybe he fell ill, too sick to call and postpone? Have you been in contact with your friends to see if he sent a message?"

"I'm heading back there as soon as I hang up with you."

"Call me when you learn what's what?"

"Of course, but wait a minute. How are you really? I mean aside from the daily routine there—are you enjoying it at all?"

Since Parke had already had enough bad news for one day, Alyx replied, "Great. Grace is great."

"Isn't she? How are her ears? Does she need her medicine?"

"Swabbed her last night, Parke. All is well."

Her cousin took a few shallow breaths. "Yes, of course. Thanks, Alyx. Are you really okay? Is the therapy helping?"

"Well, I'm not certain about Grace's, but as for me, after a rough start, Sharleigh and I have made peace and have found a good working relationship. Professionally speaking, she's still a bit too young not to get on my nerves—"

"She's you at twenty-six. Okay, without the law degree, and with a priority for snaring a wealthy husband—preferably someone established in sports or medicine—"

You're telling me, Alyx thought. "She definitely makes sure she gets first dibs on any new men coming in."

"But she's helping you? You're getting more movement out of the arm? The pain is easing?"

"Good grief, this is turning into an inquisition," Alyx said, glancing at the clock. She wasn't scheduled for therapy today, which meant she intended to take Grace for a long walk before it grew too hot for the old girl's tender paws.

"Sorry," Parke continued. "I just keep thinking I hear some hesitation in your voice—that's not the term you lawyers would lock in on, but it'll have to do. Suffice it to say that I get the feeling that you're not telling me something."

Her equally privacy-loving cousin might not be a modern-day Jane Austen with language, but there was nothing wrong with her intuition. Alyx wondered if she should tell her about Jonas? Something would have to be said about the incident with the grocery manager's nephew. No doubt the manager would mention the "friend" who had rescued her, and it wouldn't be fair to leave Parke in the dark having to grapple with figuring out the right response to make to the man.

"Okay," she said, hoping to shorthand this. "As luck would have it, I ran into someone I know from back in Texas."

"Is that what I'm hearing? He's there?"

"What, here? Now? Of course not! And why do you assume I'm talking about a 'he'?"

"I like to think we're both perceptive women, cousin. If you were referring to a woman friend, you'd have already mentioned her. So how did this reunion occur?"

"I'll tell you when you get back." Only last month Alyx had learned that the latest communication technology could allow you to eavesdrop on a conversation going on in the next car through your own mechanism. This week she'd learned that the most secretive agency in the government was recording all phone conversations in over a dozen cities. Although she and Parke were two continents and oceans apart, for all she knew some ten-year-old electronics wizard could bounce a beam off Grace's rabies tag and look up her nightshirt. She was taking no chances mentioning Jonas's own government connections. "Frankly, you'll be bored," she added, hoping to diminish some of Parke's curiosity, "and that's no way to spend your international minutes."

"At least assure me that you were nice to him?"

Alyx moaned. "Please, Parke. You've obviously inherited the few romantic genes not pickled in gin and Scotch in the family. There's nothing happening, nor is there going to be…but I do appreciate the interest," she added, prompted by her abiding respect and love for her cousin.

"You should have invited him to dinner."

"No dinner. We did open a bottle of your pinot noir. I promise to replace it by the time you get back."

"You don't have to if you tell me that you let him stay until it was finished?"

"Parke, Gracie is eyeing your Persian rug as though it's nice, thick golf turf."

"I don't own a Per—okay, I'll stop."

"And I'm hanging up to make sure you do. Love you, cousin. Good luck with Uncle No-Show."

As Alyx disconnected, she drawled to Grace, "Your mother. Let's get outside and do something constructive."

Jonas decided he could wait for Alyx to take him up on his invitation to meet again. It was important to him that she make the decision and choose the time on her own, but by closing time at the airport on Saturday, he found himself disappointed. She'd remained incommunicado; therefore, he had to assume that she was still hiding behind scars— literal and psychological. If he'd been back at his desk in Washington, D.C., he could bury himself in work and wait for exhaustion to make him not care anymore. Here, the much lighter schedule left him with too much time to ponder...and yearn.

And too much lust, he amended, with his usual need to be honest with himself.

As he locked up the hangar and shut off the fluorescent lights, he turned to finish locking up the front office only to find young Miranda standing by the doorway. Her slinky purse strap was slung over a bare shoulder, the tight, off-the-shoulder top and her matching white, rhinestone-studded jeans looked more appropriate for a disco or a spur-of-the-moment Vegas wedding than an airport office. Jonas knew he had to get out of there.

Miranda had been doing her best to tempt him with her *assets* since his arrival—even Alyx had figured that much out—and today the kid was clearly going for broke. He wanted no part of what he suspected was going on in her one-track mind, and hoped he could get her out of here without having to hurt her feelings or embarrass himself.

"Miranda, you're still here? You should have felt free to cut out early." Did he sound anywhere close to paternal as he'd hoped? "As slow as it's been what with the plane trouble this week, no need to waste more of your personal time than necessary sitting behind that counter."

"I didn't want to go while you were still up in one of the planes." Offering him a dazzling smile, she asked, "How about you let me buy you a drink? You'd be rescuing me from a family dinner that I can only miss if I have a good excuse."

Groaning inwardly, Jonas gestured for her to go ahead into the reception area, then he locked the door to the hangar. "That couldn't possibly be me, kiddo. You'll have to dig deeper into your cell phone's address book for younger companionship. I'm going to take my weary bones to Zane's place and sleep until the next sunrise." Although he was restless, not tired, Jonas made the point of acting the part as he checked to make sure the bathrooms were empty. When he returned to her, he held out his hand. "Deposit bag?"

Looking more than a little miffed, Miranda dropped it onto his palm as though not wanting to contaminate herself by touching him. "You don't know what you'll be missing," she said with all of the haughtiness only someone her age could manage.

"Oh, but I do—I'm going to miss the chance of your family finding out and your father coming after me with a tire iron or worse. I'm old enough to be your father." He grasped her elbow and urged her to the front door. "Have a great evening and I'll see you on Monday."

With an insulted huff, Miranda strode off to her car never looking back.

"Round two—Hunter," he declared under his breath. He didn't believe for a moment that this was the end of Miss Miranda's attempts to lasso his attention, despite his having hoped he'd quelled her interest earlier in the week. Young she might be, but Alyx was right about her; Miranda was one of those women who clamped on to people the way most bloodsuckers did their hosts, refusing to let go until she'd consumed every ounce of life from them.

Pitying Miranda's next target and hoping Zane's broken leg healed faster than estimated, he climbed into the vintage Mustang and checked for messages on his Black-Berry. There was nothing from his son, Blake, or from Alyx, only a few interoffice memos from the Agency that he would automatically get, regardless of whether he was in-office or on the road. Blake's silence didn't concern him too much. About to turn fifteen, his technology-insatiable kid did well to know what day it was and to get to school on time. Grasping that an absent parent cared to know what new gizmo he'd turned into his latest favorite playground wouldn't occur to the left-brainer who lived happily in his own head. Thank goodness these days he could count on Claudia to let him know if something was seriously amiss. After a few rough months in the beginning of their separation, their divorce had become amicable, no small thanks to her being happy in her second marriage.

When he got to Zane's airy adobe-style home, Jonas let

himself inside to find his groaning friend being helped back onto the couch by a small, plump woman with short and spiky eggplant-colored hair.

"Whoa—wait, Betty!" He dashed to help. "Watch your back with that big loaf of bread." He got to them in time to help ease his well-muscled friend down onto their big sectional couch. "What happened?" he asked as Zane groaned.

"He tripped getting the mail," Betty replied breathlessly. "I told him I'd get it. I told him that the sidewalk wasn't wide enough for him and his crutches both, but did he listen?"

"I listened," Zane groaned.

"What Mr. Denial did was slip off into the garden rock. I think he pinched a nerve and probably injured a few muscles and tendons in his good leg trying to save the cast."

Just the image of that had Jonas wincing. He cast his friend a doubtful look. "You are *trying* to get better, aren't you?"

They'd been friends for about twenty years, first meeting at the FBI Academy. When Zane left after a few years in the program, he'd gone to fly for a major freight company. Next thing Jonas heard, he'd bought an Internet stock low, sold it high, and left the risky world of rain-snow-sleet deliveries-via-wing-and-prayer to start his own airline business—such as it was.

"Stuff it, Hunter," Zane grumbled. "I'm supposed to do more at this stage than sit here and grow mold."

Betty asked Jonas, "Do you think he should go in for X-rays? He fell so hard on his arm."

"Oh, he's probably gained enough weight since sitting around on his big butt to have buffered any threat to those bones," Jonas told her, enjoying the murderous look his friend shot him. "What do you think, old man? Want us to haul you down to the clinic for that? Where does it hurt most?"

"In my ego."

"Chronic but not terminal," Betty said to Jonas.

"Then if you don't mind, I'll scram," Jonas said to both of them. "I just meant to poke my head in to ask if I could borrow the car for a while longer?"

"Of course." Ignoring Zane's narrow-eyed scrutiny, Betty patted Jonas's arm. "It's about time you took some time to enjoy yourself. He sure won't need it tonight." To her husband she added, "I'm going to make you some tortilla soup."

Watching her leave, Zane's expression went from pained to determined. "Quick," he whispered when she was gone. "Get me that bottle of tequila on the bar."

"You know I can't do that."

"You would if you'd tasted her soup."

Jonas chuckled. "I'll pour you a drink, but then you're on your own."

Chapter Seven

The house was too quiet. Why weren't there any squad cars here yet? Alyx would never have thought to venture out of her car, let alone knock at the door, but there was only Cassandra's white Toyota Camry in the driveway. Maybe it was all over and Cassie's estranged husband had been hauled off to jail?

"Cass?"

Hearing nothing, Alyx tested the doorknob. It turned easily. That would be like her client to be so shaken by Douglas that she forgot to lock up after he'd been taken away by the police.

Stepping inside, she called again, "Cassandra? It's Alyx—are you all right?"

The prolonged silence was unnerving, yet she took a second step inside, and from the corner of her left eye saw *a dark spot on the floor…a dark spot that was expanding. Just as that spot registered in her mind as blood, Alyx heard sirens.*

Sirens only now?

When they'd talked earlier, Douglas was beating on the door, and she'd told Cass to hang up immediately and call 911 to initiate the GPS tracking. Then as she'd run to her car—leaving Dylan's swearing-in ceremony—she'd called 911, too, to back up that alert.

With the dreaded realization that her client probably hadn't had time for that call, Alyx rushed around the counter corner only to stop in midstep as the contents of her stomach lurched up into her throat.

"Oh, God! Cassie—"

The door shut behind her with an eerie click.

Spinning around, Alyx saw Douglas Conroe, soaked in his estranged wife's blood…and the knife he'd used on her was gripped in his right hand.

He was six feet tall and well over two hundred pounds; the idea of fighting Doug was laughable. Alyx knew her best chance was escape, or to keep him from inflicting too much damage before the police reached them.

"Always conniving," he sneered.

"Put the knife down, Douglas. The police will be easier with you if you surrender willingly."

"You think I care? I'm here to finish business."

Alyx wanted to run, but her feet refused to cooperate. She wanted to scream, but no willpower she possessed could force anything past the block of terror shutting her throat.

"No—" she thought as he stepped toward her. Spinning away, she swept up a casserole dish. For a moment Doug-

las hesitated. She knew he expected her to throw it at him, but an inexplicable inspiration made her throw it with all of her might at the kitchen window. Shards of glass and pottery flew inside and out and the noise startled her as much as it did Cassandra's husband. *Please let that get the police in here faster,* she thought.

With his glazed eyes seething hatred, Douglas lunged at her.

Alyx screamed and dodged to get out of his reach, then found the strength to run, but misjudged the corner and banged her hip so hard the pain stole her breath as badly as it threw her off balance. That was all Douglas needed to drive the knife into her shoulder.

The pain all but dropped her to her knees. Blindly grabbing at whatever was in reach, she threw it back at him. That was enough to make him back off a moment and she ran again. But he wasn't thwarted for long.

"No!" she screamed again and again as he slashed repeatedly. She was going to die. Knew she was going to...

"Alyx, stop! It's me—it's *me!*"

Suddenly Jonas was before her, gripping her wrists and gasping for breath—and there was blood, *blood* on him, too!

"Did you kill him?"

"It's all right, Alyx. You were dreaming."

Blinking, she glanced around. At first she didn't recognize the room, but then she saw the cactus sculpture on the coffee table that Parke had created. She wasn't in Texas. Yet even as embarrassment set in, she focused on the confusion about why Jonas was here.

She reached for his face. "You're bleeding..."

"The glass fought back."

"What?"

"Bad joke." Grimacing, he sat down beside her on the couch and without asking for permission wrapped his arms around her. "I'd just arrived and heard your screams—I'm sorry. I thought the worst and broke in. Don't worry, the window will be replaced as soon as I clean up."

She had no doubt his word was good, she was simply trying to figure out something. Easing away from him, she searched his face again. "But what are you doing here?"

He averted his eyes and busied himself, using his shirt to wipe the blood trickling down his arm and fingers. "It was one of those things." Rubbing harder, he admitted, "I felt funny."

"As in, I'm going to find this hilarious?"

"More like having a feeling that you weren't okay."

What an odd admission, since they'd both agreed during one of their rare, deeper conversations that didn't involve foreplay that they didn't buy into the precognitive, hocus-pocus stuff. With a nod toward the hallway she said, "Please, let's get you cleaned up. You have to be in pain, too. Do you think any of the cuts are going to need stitches?"

"A couple of pressure bandages should do the trick." Despite his injuries, Jonas offered a hand to help her to her feet. "Alyx, you're still in shock, but you need to reassure Grace," he said when they were close enough to exchange breaths. "She ran from the room when I burst in."

Grace—of course! Alyx gained strength from having something else to focus on. "Poor girl. Everything is upside down for her. We haven't had enough time to really bond, and I'm not a coddling type to begin with."

She admired Grace's record as a racer, but she'd never had the delusions that Parke did—that a dog bred just for running fast would be a good companion, never mind protect its second, third—or was it fourth?—owner in the presence of harm? Thank goodness the question still didn't need answering.

"Alyx, could we save the introspection for when I'm not ruining your cousin's furniture on top of her entry-way?"

Startled again out of her stupor, Alyx led the way down the hall. In the glistening pine-and-brass-adorned bathroom, she got a roll of paper towels out of a cabinet for Jonas, knowing he would be loathe to use one of her cousin's honey-and-cream towels. From another cabinet she got out peroxide, antibiotic ointment and bandages. "I'll be back in a minute to help you with that," she said before dashing down the hall again to check on Grace.

"Take your time," Jonas called behind her.

Alyx found Grace on Parke's bed with her nose tucked under the pillows.

"Oh. Gracious, Grace, I am sorry." Alyx sat down beside her and stroked her back. There was no missing the subtle trembling she felt there. "I know I must have scared you witless and then to see the glass break, too… You want your lady back in the worst way. I wish I could bring her home to you sooner. But I promise you that I'll do my best to do better until she's here, okay?"

The dog sighed, then after a moment lifted her head and looked at Alyx. Alyx didn't know when she'd seen a more sincere attempt to convey entreaty.

"I swear if you actually spoke right now, I wouldn't need

a translator," she told her. "Yes, I meant what I said. Let me go help Jonas and I'll get you a biscuit. Want a biscuit?"

Grace bounded off the bed and trotted to the kitchen.

Alyx followed and at the bathroom door said, "Only one more minute. How's the bleeding?"

"Haven't run completely out yet."

The man intended to go down a comedian. "I'm giving her a treat since she's willing to forgive me."

"Sure."

As she continued down the hallway, Alyx felt heat flood places that had felt dead for months. She'd definitely made herself forget that Jonas Hunter was eye candy in his so-obvious government employee suit and double that in any state of undress. Passing the open door and seeing him naked from the waist up had stirred her temperature to where she was wondering if she'd already begun those menopausal hot flashes.

"Biscuits…focus on doggie treats." She got two treats for Grace and as an afterthought added ice cubes to the canine's water bowl. Parke had informed her that Grace liked ice water as much as humans did, plus the colder temperatures reduced the growth of bacteria in this warm environment.

Assured the dog was content for the moment, Alyx forced herself to return to Jonas. But a second glance at the mess in the entryway was keeping her stressed and uneasy.

How could she not have wakened as he'd broken in? She had to have been deep in sleep, which didn't bode well for her state of mind. It also wouldn't be easy to replace that custom-cut frosted pane beside the door.

Upon entering the bathroom, she saw he was dressed again, but in the half-soaked shirt. The navy-blue color might have hidden it, but she knew that there'd been a good deal of blood in it. "You don't have to do that," she told him. "Take that shirt off and let's clean it properly. I'm sure that I can find you something else to wear while it dries."

"It'll do that quickly enough once I'm outside," he told her with equal casualness. "But if you could help with the gauze to wrap this arm bandage, I'd appreciate that. I'm clearly short a couple of hands."

There was an understatement. She could already see signs of bleeding through the pads. Dropping all pretenses that she could take this in stride, she stayed his hand. "Jonas—this doesn't look good. I'd feel so much better if you let me take you to the clinic."

"I'll go have Zane's wife, Betty, do it."

Why was he being like this? "All right, all right. It's your blood. Excuse me for being concerned."

Jonas settled back against the vanity and cradled his elbow on the arm wrapped around his waist. "I appreciate that, but it's not bad. More important is that you don't—"

"Don't what?"

"Well, regress."

As soon as he spoke those words, he wished he could take them back. The back stiffening would have been enough to sound internal alarms, but when that was followed by her arching her eyebrows, Jonas considered tearing off the bandages to let himself bleed to death. It might be an easier end.

"I had a bad dream," she enunciated quietly. "They come less frequently than before, thank you. How is that sabotaging myself?"

Jonas closed his eyes. "I'm male. I never get it right the first time. You're the gifted orator. What do I say to fix this?"

"You say *nothing*…and you let Defense hug you to keep you from injuring yourself further."

Who was he to pass up a directive like that? Relieved that she wasn't ordering him out, he carefully embraced her, concerned that some bleed-through would stain her buttery-yellow silk shirt.

Then he stopped worrying. Feeling her womanly curves against him reminded him of why he'd spent a small bundle over Thanksgiving and Christmas on airline tickets to be with her, although she'd kept insisting that she wouldn't be getting into a serious relationship with him or anyone. All she'd offered was sex, which had been terrific, but increasingly not enough to him. He'd never challenged or argued with her. His MO had been discreetly to win more of her time.

"What is that scent you wear?" he finally had to ask. The memory of it had been haunting him for all of the months that they'd been apart; however, when she just stared at him, he was forced to ask, "What?"

"I'm not sure whether you really mean that or you think you need to be nice?"

Since when did a compliment deserve such scrutiny? "That's no question to ask."

"Then you've been living in a closet. These days when most men mention a woman's scent it's to complain that it's too strong."

"That can't be true."

"Excuse me, it happened to *me*. The last time I flew somewhere, I had a discreet touch to my wrists and behind my knees that I'd put on almost two hours earlier—"

Jonas felt his body react to the sensual mention of touching a perfume stopper to the backs of her knees. He already knew from experience where she'd put fragrance and suspected he dreamed about it as well.

"—but as I stood in line at the airport, some smart-mouth right behind me trying to impress his buddy started talking about perfumes. Smells he could stand and the clogging of his nostrils that was—and I quote—'about to kill him.'"

"Not everyone is gifted in verbal expression."

"Smelled."

"Did you at least pay for his funeral?"

"No, but I did take a long look at him to make sure he wasn't a former client's ex—just in case I needed to worry about a sham restraining order. Then I told him—with admirable restraint—that if his head wasn't stuck where it was, the equipment he was born with would operate with greater reliability."

This Jonas believed. Aside from being a she-tiger when it came to defending her clients, Alyx didn't handle males being fools in public well, either—but she sure seemed to attract her share of them. "Did he grasp what you were telling him?"

"No." Then she smiled. "But the man who was seeing him off—no doubt having endured his own experiences with him—put a hand over the jerk's mouth and said, 'Trust me. Go...*and live to speak of this another day.*'"

"Not only a wise man, but one with a sense of humor." Jonas couldn't always tell whether she was being delightful to put him at ease, or scarily honest. "Well, my vital signs are at your mercy, but regardless, your scent is lovely. I liked it from the first and I've missed it."

Alyx gave him another skeptical look, but offered, "It's an old faithful. Number five."

"Chanel? No wonder I keep having visions of Audrey Hepburn and Grace Kelly movies. I'm a sucker for the old romantic classics."

She leaned closer to whisper into his ear, "Personally, I can't get enough serial-killer flicks, particularly the night before a court appearance."

When she also eased out of his arms and put some distance between them, Jonas came to the conclusion that he'd perfected his lady-killer, Cary Grant–persona at the cost of making him poisonous to a certain kind of woman—the woman that he was realizing, with increased certainty, he wanted. Who would have thought that flattery would be a bad thing?

Smart enough to resist trying to resume the hug, he replied, "My hunch is that you'd prefer Hitchcock, but when do you have time for that? I remember your house having towers of case files piled all over."

"Ah, well, I have to confess…I would keep some boxes of closed cases in closets to lay out in case a boring or no-holds-barred *bad* date needed a stronger hint to leave."

Jonas didn't want to think of how long the confession list might be. "Stop anytime you want to."

Taking up the roll of gauze, Alyx replied, "After I add that maybe with you the stacked work was current."

"Nice save."

"And you were by far the least annoying dinner date."

She was wicked and enjoyed every second of it. He could see how her thick eyelashes fluttered as she fought her desire to see what he thought of her every poke at his ego.

Brushing her hair behind her shoulder so he could keep analyzing her, Jonas felt compelled to disclose a little of what he suspected. "You try so hard to be a hard case."

"I am a bit off my stride. But don't think I won't be back in rare form soon enough."

He wanted to laugh, knowing that was a truth for sure. Yet a sigh came first. "You scared the crap out of me, Alyx. I mean when I heard you scream a few minutes ago."

"Well, apparently I scared myself, too."

"Will you let me in on what prompted that dream?"

Frowning, she immediately set to attending to the wound on his forearm. "I would if I knew."

"Does that mean you're not ready to tell me yet?"

"This bandage may be too tight."

"I think the consensus is the tighter the better."

"Good. But I don't know if flying is going to be a smart idea for the next day or so. Is there much muscle strain in handling those planes?"

"Nothing I can't handle."

"Jonas, good pilots are in graveyards all over the blessed planet."

He caressed her cheek with the backs of his fingers. "Alyx—keep dodging if you want, but I'll keep asking the question."

"Okay, okay." She drew a deep breath as though preparing for an aria, only to yield with a sigh. "There wasn't anything negative; in fact, this week I was heartened that I seemed to be doing so much better, not only with rehab, but I haven't been waking in the middle of the night in a cold sweat."

"That's great news."

Finished with his arm, Alyx fussed over the Band-Aid on his forehead that was already coming loose. "Better anyway."

"Maybe that's a sign that you need to continue letting your guard down a little more."

"You think? G-man, that's what got me in this condition." Lifting her sardonic gaze to meet his, she added, "And look who's talking—Mr. Ask Me No Questions so I Don't Have to Spin Tall Tales."

"I don't recall you asking me anything that I couldn't answer."

Alyx didn't yield a centimeter. Nose to nose, she countered, "That's because I wasn't interested in any classified information—and the only personal question about your life I needed to know about was if you'd had a recent health check."

How many times did she think it was fair to wound a guy? "What was I to you, a mere sex object? In the beginning, okay. But—" He had to stop before he said something that made him sound even more stupid. Good grief, he felt like a male blond joke. "*Why* do you think I made all of those trips down to Austin?" he asked her, still not able to believe what she was telling him.

"You said you were working on cases."

"Every few weekends? Over holidays? Come on, Alyx. We spent every spare minute you had together, didn't that give you a clue?"

In the reverberating silence Jonas suspected he'd gone too far. Raising his voice could have reminded her of Cassandra's husband...or maybe her father, or both.

"So I'm an awful person because you're realizing that there are women who don't live and breathe to trap you into a wedding proposal?"

Sometimes there was nothing left to do but cut to the important thing. Jonas knew important—the feeling of his lips touched hers. Clasping his hand behind her head, he claimed her mouth with his.

It would be a lie to deny there wasn't some anger at first. The woman could wear out a water buffalo with her determination not to yield an inch of ground once she felt she was right. But the feel of her pliable, silken lips, combined with her taste, soon made him push the rest out of his mind. That was a humbling experience as well.

Relief came when he slanted his head and sought a deeper kiss. Finally she gripped his shoulders and responded with equal hunger, their tongues colliding and stroking in a sudden frenzy of yearning, more intense because of familiarity. As sensations ricocheted through him, he slipped his arm around her waist to draw her closer to where heat and need ignited first. Sweet heaven, he'd missed this, her. When she arched closer to his inevitable arousal, he groaned, already remembering the last time they'd been together, naked, and as one.

"I miss you so damned much I hurt," he rasped.

"Jonas…Jonas…this is crazy."

"Crazy is good if it feels like this."

As quickly as she began pulling away, Alyx clung to him again and kissed him as though it was their first passion all over. Breathing was forgotten. Injuries were an aside. They could have been Shakespeare's youngest lovers in those few tempestuous, healing seconds. Torturous moments because they couldn't last.

The instant she accepted that truth, Alyx pushed him away with an anguished, "No!"

"Why not?" Jonas asked between shallow breaths.

"Because I've worked too hard to get my head straight to lose myself in you again."

Again? Had he managed to get a confession out of her after all? "We can take things at your pace." That was laughable since his body had just told her otherwise. "If anyone understands, it's me."

"That's one way to look at it, I suppose. The other is that you've already got one failed marriage on your résumé, you work for a government agency that is as likely as not to stick you in some forsaken place, or worse, get you killed."

"Well, I hate to bring this up, sweetheart, but you've come closer to that probability than I have."

"That was a low blow."

"No, it was honest—something we could use a little more of around each other."

"I have been honest. I've asked for nothing from you, and I've thanked you repeatedly for your company."

"You haven't asked for anything, out of fear," Jonas snapped. "You're afraid of being rejected or left behind."

Alyx stiffened. "I'm done with this conversation. You've got the wrong woman. I'm not the commitment kind, let alone the marrying kind, and even if I were, you'd be the last man I'd consider."

Chapter Eight

It was a good thing that Jonas needed to leave to find suitable glass to replace the one he'd ruined—at least until someone could create the real thing for Parke. Alyx needed time to recover from her outburst.

The look on his face would not be easy to forget. But it had been panic that made her blurt out what she did. He'd had no business forcing that confrontation.

Nevertheless, when he returned almost ninety minutes later, she was relieved. A part of her had feared he'd hire someone to do the job at any cost to avoid having to face her again. Goodness, considering his cuts, she should have insisted.

"Can I help you get it out of the car and set into the frame?" she asked him, now that she was thinking more clearly.

"That'll be fine."

"Better yet, let me call for tradesmen to deal with this. If you open that deepest cut—"

"I won't."

Alyx winced at his formal tone but was glad he accepted her assistance; the job would have been nearly impossible for one person trying to solo it. Thank goodness Jonas had some skills as a handyman, as well. He was caulking the new pane in place in no time.

"I'm impressed," she told him.

"Be sure to tell your cousin that I'm good for the real thing whenever she decides what she wants."

"She's going to understand, Jonas." Besides, Alyx saw it as her fault that he'd felt a need to break in, and she would be handling the expense herself. Stripping off the gloves she'd put on to help move and hold the glass, she added, "Would you like a beer or glass of wine? You have to be thirsty. How about ice water?"

"That's okay. I'm sure you're ready to see the last of me."

She was ready for her life to begin resembling something that felt comfortable—and this sure wasn't it. "What I'm ready for is a glass of wine—and you said you want to wait and see that the caulk holds, so I'm getting you a glass, too."

As she poured, Alyx took comfort in the fact that Jonas hadn't rejected the offer outright. He'd had every right to. But since he was here, she could at least try to make him understand that her rejection might have been mostly reaction, but her mindset wasn't about him—she was simply the square peg not fitting in the round hole.

She found him sitting on the biggest garden rock out front. "Please come inside and cool off," she said as she held both glasses. "The caulk won't dry any faster with you watching it, while you bake out here. Our ancestors said as much."

"I don't exactly remember that old saying."

"Remember 'a watched pot never boils'? Same logic."

"So even out of the courtroom you've got a comment on everything."

"I had a professor in law school who was like no one in the business. He reminded me of a high-school general business teacher I'd had. You didn't just learn the mechanics, you got homilies, anecdotes, his personal history…it was all about understanding that most of the people you met in the courtroom might not be like you on one or several levels. They came with their own baggage. The better you were at drawing out that information, the more likely you'd get a jury you wanted. Even though I didn't go into trial law, I never forgot those classes."

Accepting the glass, Jonas murmured, "It shows." He cast her a dubious glance. "You're okay with that?"

"You coming inside? Don't be silly. Besides, I need to watch about too much sun. I'm part vampire if you haven't already figured that out." She didn't quite make him laugh, but he followed her inside where she led him to Parke's studio. "I didn't get to show you this the other day. When I have trouble sleeping, I come here."

Jonas stopped in his tracks and gaped. "Damn."

"Exactly."

Everything here was a work in progress. Parke worked in moods and she needed breaks between commissions to revive her body and spirit. Four projects in the cathedral-like room were in various stages of completion. That was the maximum overbooking she would allow herself out of concern about disappointing a client. One work was a twelve-foot-tall cemetery monument to honor a soldier-son; the second was a fountain to enhance a bird-lover's garden; the third was a tribute to a granddaughter taken from her family and the fourth was confusing because it was still in several pieces.

"It's to be a part of a vast hotel waterfall," Alyx told him. "At this stage it seems like something out of *Peter Pan,* doesn't it?"

"I think it does." Jonas sipped his wine and did a solo walk around the room. "At the end of a life involving work like this, you can't say you're clueless as to what you've accomplished."

"No, you can't."

He returned to her side. "So you two are close?"

"Strange as it might seem we are, in an oddly scheduled kind of way. We won't speak for a month, then one day she'll call with a need for a dog-and-house sitter, and… here I am because I realized I was in a need of a change of scenery."

"This is a paternal cousin?"

"No, my mother's sister's only child. It seems they both chose badly when it came to life partners."

"Am I supposed to say, 'No wonder you don't want anything to do with relationships'?"

"I suppose you could, and I suspect there's an ounce or pound of truth in that depending on whether you believe that nature or nurture has the prevalent influence in our lives."

"And you believe?"

"That I'm off the clock and with no one relying on me for my judgment, I don't have one…or I don't care to dwell, explain, defend or worry about it. I simply wanted you to see Parke's talent."

She figured she owed him. That's why she'd brought him back into the house, back here where Parke's energy was at its most visual. Her cousin was more open and maybe if she could channel some of that energy, she and Jonas could make peace so there would be no more hard feelings. It was as simple as that.

"And I thought I was facing burnout."

The possibility had occurred to her. Early in her career she'd dealt with a number of public defenders and that burnout ratio had been frightening. Since then she'd seen how many people in almost every area of law or law enforcement had to deal with moments when they questioned, "What's it all about?" and "Do I want to continue doing this until I retire…if I make it that long?" He might be in a loftier agency with more respect and clout, but it probably wasn't any different for agents like him, either.

Pausing by the back doors that overlooked a hiker's trail and more red-rock monuments, Alyx noted how the color of her wine against the backdrop of cactus, earth and sky not only worked together, but made her feel one with this environment.

"I'm not burned out, Jonas. I still believe in keeping people like E.D. from getting mauled by the predators that use the legal system for profit. But I am grateful I can take this break without having to hear whispers from back home that I've signed myself into some luxury rehab place."

When he arrived beside her, he leaned against the wood of the French doors and studied her profile, not the exquisite scenery outside. "Can I ask again if you're in a lot of pain?"

"This dry heat has been a relief, and the therapy has me at about eighty-five-percent mobility. Losing almost six pounds hasn't hurt, either."

"You didn't need to lose weight, Alyx."

"My designer suits would tell you otherwise."

"Sure, shatter my cleavage fantasy."

"I was endowed amply enough in that department," she replied, patting his chest as she began to return to the kitchen. "Sometimes more isn't more."

"No, in your case it's perfect." With a smooth turn, Jonas blocked her way and, searching her eyes, he noted, "Yes, everything is healing—except for your hearing."

What was she supposed to do? When he was close like this, her lips tingled with the need to feel them pressed to his again, her fingers itched to touch him. Like any couple that had been intimate numerous times, they each knew the other's body as well as their own. She hadn't wanted to think about it, but there was no escaping reality when they stood this close. Hadn't he said it himself? "We fit."

"Kiss me," he murmured. "Call it a goodbye, or no hard feelings, or—damn the reasons, just—"

She did. Lifting her chin, she touched her lips to his and savored his surprise and subsequent pleasure. Then, like someone parched with thirst, he pressed closer to drink in all of her that he could.

It wasn't fair to be reminded of what she'd been missing, what she was determined to give up. But one way or another, saying goodbye was the reasonable thing to do. He was at a crossroads himself, clearly moving on, even though he didn't know to what or to where. Forced by life's circumstances and admitted personal decisions, they were heading in different directions. Maybe in that case it wasn't crazy to be a little indulgent this one last time.

Alyx put all of herself into the kiss and that was a pleasure in itself. She'd never been able to let down her guard totally with a lover—not until Jonas. They were still strangers in many, no, in most, ways, yet in bed, they seemed to know each other effortlessly. She would never forget him and had lain awake many a night wishing for him. But, better that, she concluded, than to have never experienced such sensual perfection.

"There you go thinking again," Jonas said against her forehead as he struggled to catch his breath.

"I was in danger of letting this glass slip from my fingers and I know how expensive these are—I sent them to Parke as a housewarming present when she moved out here."

"What a lovely compliment." He angled his head to nuzzle her ear, only to nip at her diamond stud earring. "I like knowing I might be able to make you lose control."

"You always could, from that first night." She remembered the heat that had raced through her body when they'd followed E.D. and Dylan out of her office building and Jonas had retraced his steps, pretending to need to ask her another question. However, what he'd done was to ask her out for a drink, while his gaze had boldly offered more. "Do you think E.D. and Dylan knew what was happening between us?" she asked, before letting the last sip of wine slide down her parched throat.

"They only had eyes for each other."

"He never asked you later?"

"Nope. Too much of a gentleman. When we were young Turks, he might have, but only if we'd been alone." Jonas brushed his lips along her jaw. "It's a little late to worry about it now."

"I'm not worried." She doubted it would have changed things anyway. Desire had never come so quickly or been so completely consuming. She'd just wondered if that had radiated from her as powerfully as she suspected it did. That relentless craving for him was back again and she knew her lacy bra was exposing that through her silk blouse.

Never one to miss much, Jonas brushed his knuckles over one taut bud, and Alyx couldn't hide the soft hitch in her breathing, or the shiver that sped through her. When Jonas kissed her again, she let her body gravitate to his, the need to ease a deep ache stronger than her willpower to be sensible.

Jonas rewarded her with a low groan. "That is more delicious than any wine every created." Blindly reaching out, he set his empty glass on a workstation, then cupped her hips and rocked himself slowly and repeatedly against her.

To keep herself from ripping at the neckline of his shirt and pressing her lips there, Alyx sought another kiss. He responded with even greater hunger, his tongue matching the rhythm of his hips until she could feel herself melting, and hear her pounding heartbeat echoing in her cars.

"Damn, Alyx," Jonas rasped. "In another second I'm going to ruin your reputation and maybe your cousin's by pulling one of these tarps to the floor and dragging you down on top of it—joggers and birdwatchers with binoculars be warned."

Almost mournfully, she told him, "If it was a moonless night, and I was twenty-something, I might let you."

"Lady, you don't need to hide anything. You're hotter than any androgynous kid, and will be at seventy-something."

"In that case, I just remembered I need to feed Grace."

"Speaking of skeletons…what's that take, a deboned chicken wing and three kernels of dry dog food?"

It was time, Alyx knew, to take hold of his hand and lead him to the kitchen. She even began to say, "Come *on*. I'll pour you another wine if—"

Jonas didn't let her finish. Leading her away from the windows, he brought her to an antique chaise longue behind a workbench, obviously where Parke rested when she needed time to study the possibilities of a piece…or to hide from the intimidation of it. Jonas's mind was too fixated on other possibilities to give that anything other than cursory thought.

"What are you doing?" Alyx cried as he grabbed a sheet and tossed it over the couch.

"You know."

"That's insane. Even if we could, you'll open those cuts."

"Then be gentle with me." With a smile turning his blue eyes almost silver, he silenced her with another kiss. Maybe he was pushing his luck, he thought as he plucked her glass from her fingers, but he figured he had nothing to lose. If he let her send him away this time, he had a hunch her determination would compound and there would never be a next time. Now that she'd let him touch her, taste her again, he had to have everything.

By the time he'd put the glass out of harm's way and had her stretched across the chaise, they were both breathing shallowly and she was staring at him with wide-eyed incredulity. Ignoring that, he unbuttoned her blouse to the waistband of her slacks. She had the most glorious honey-

and-cream skin that all but cried out to be caressed and kissed. He did both, lingering with pleasure to brush his lips from the swell of her right breast down into the damp valley where her heart was thudding and up across her left breast.

"You're so beautiful," he murmured. His hot breath warmed her through her lacy bra, not surprisingly teasing her rosy nipple into a tight bead.

Alyx self-consciously drew her blouse back by the collar to keep her wounds hidden from him. "Jonas—"

"Don't," he entreated. "You have to know I understand, and the only thing I'll be seeing is your bravery." Bending to her, he nudged the cloth aside with his nose, then brushed a kiss from her breast upward, until his lips reached the first feathery line forever cut into her perfect skin. The surgeons had taken their time trying not only to repair what that monster had done to her, but to remove as many signs of the inevitable scar tissue as possible. Even at this early date, Jonas thought they'd done an impressive and appreciable job.

Aware she was staring off into space waiting for him to lie or leave, Jonas said simply, "It looks like a piece of a star fell to earth to leave its white-hot kiss on you." Gently touching his lips to the center where the diagonal lines seemed to merge, he met Alyx's gaze, only to see a hint of tears shimmer in her eyes.

"You're a sweet liar, Jonas." Framing his head with her hands, she drew down his head to hers.

Her natural voice was seductive—more alto than second soprano, and she lacked any drawl despite being a native-born Texan. Vulnerability and perhaps desire brought richer notes to it that stirred a unique protectiveness in him, just as it heated the yearning in his belly. In the slow, thorough kiss they shared, he tried to show her that he hadn't lied much, hardly a bit.

The yearning had to be mutual because he felt her arch her hips to get closer to him, and he eased his right leg between her thighs to increase that sensation while taking some of his weight off her injured thigh. Then he shifted his mouth to her lace-covered breast and drew her taut nipple into his mouth.

Her reaction was as sudden and fierce as his; her fingers raked into his hair to clutch him closer, while the rest of her trembled with an almost virginal reaction. If he could, he would have confessed that he'd been without any sexual contact for as long as she'd all but confessed, and that being with the only woman he wanted was nearly frying his brain. But it was getting tough enough to breathe, let alone speak and when Alyx shoved his polo shirt up under his armpits, he thumbed the snap of her bra and brought them flesh-to-flesh for yet another level of sweet torture. Their hands bumped as they attacked the fastenings on her slacks and his jeans, merely moving the clothing enough to reach each other.

Jonas drove into her with a smooth thrust. Her warm, welcoming heat nearly sent him over the edge in that instant. It had almost always been that way upon an initial reunion following some weeks apart. After that first race to pleasure, they would strive for the patience to savor and explore, but not the first time and not this time. And yet something was different for Jonas—and, maybe he imagined it because he wanted to, but he sensed a yearning in Alyx's kiss. It spoke of depth beyond predatory passions.

Like a blind man thinking he was witnessing his first glimmer of moonlight, he reached for it, for her, until, drinking in her cry, Jonas climaxed and rode blind on that fierce wave of satisfaction.

Fierce, fickle wave.

Whose voice was *that?* As his mind began to clear, Jonas wondered if he'd subconsciously channeled a movie line, or was he remembering some corny poetry he'd listened to for hours at a coffeehouse stakeout some years ago? Whatever it was, it wasn't a thought in *his* language and, yet, it hit a nerve.

Alyx would recover at any second, too, and probably push his butt off the chaise in her eagerness to wipe this experience off the day-planner of her life. Then she'd order him out—or worse. While that was the exact opposite of what he'd been thinking a moment ago, his descent back into reality succeeded in draining him of all confidence. This was, after all, Alyx Carmel, the Scarlett O'Hara of Texas law.

"Whatever you feel the need to do or say," he rasped against her hair. "Don't regret this."

Chapter Nine

No, there would be no regret.

The second Alyx had sensed a flicker of regained sanity, she'd begun to berate herself for not thinking more of Parke's reputation. Had one of the neighbors come to the back doors as she knew they were apt to do, the cul-de-sac of well-to-do retirees looking for escape from their own personal boredom would be in the thick of scandal. But that worry was short-lived. At some point between Jonas storming the front door and this resumption of their intimacy, she'd decided she couldn't help believing that she'd replaced the cold steel in her spine for legitimate bone and marrow. What happened had been with her cooperation—she had to be honest about *her* participation in this.

"No," she whispered, sensing a unique vulnerability in

him, as well. Whether imagined or not, she touched her hand to his cheek. "No regrets."

Jonas stroked her from hip to breast. "Thank you."

There was tenderness in his look and touch that kept her from knowing what to do next. Then pink caught her eye. "Jonas...the bandages! You're bleeding through." She quickly pressed back into the chaise to fasten her bra and button her blouse.

"Ah! Sorry." After adjusting his jeans, he rose and offered her his hand. "Are you okay? How's your thigh? I tried to keep my weight off it."

By putting weight on his arms, that explained why his wounds were breaking open. "Let's get you back to the bathroom."

Once there, she took control, ordering him to lean over the sink while she grabbed scissors from the drawer and cut off the saturated bandages, then collected the necessary items to get him cleaned up again. Aside from being upset that he'd refused to go to a clinic for help in the first place, this second view of so much blood was a ghastly reminder of her own wounds and her stomach threatened to revolt.

To his credit, Jonas caught on fast. "You're not about to get sick, are you?"

"There are scratches and cuts...and then there's this," she muttered between gulps of air. "Jonas, these are gashes!"

Almost whimsically, he shrugged and replied, "Just secure the bandages tighter this time, that's all."

That's all? "Fine—but then *you* need to keep your arms out from under *me!*"

Upset that he didn't get it, she decided his silence was the smartest decision he'd made in the last hour. But, as she worked, Alyx was aware that he studied her profile. She wished he would stop that, too. Those pale eyes unnerved her. She knew there were men who, if asked, "What are you thinking?" would answer, "Nothing," and be dead-on accurate. He wasn't one of those.

"I'm not angry with you," she finally blurted out.

"I know."

"It's just that you could have severed an artery bursting in like that, and you're so proud with your one-riot-one-agent attitude—"

"Wrong group, sweetheart. Those are the Texas Rangers."

She shot him a searing glance. "I know that. I'm just saying that you all think you're immortal."

"Yes. And you care, and that throws you off your life plan."

"I don't have a life plan." Not now anyway.

"At least you didn't deny that you care."

Out of the corner of her eye she saw his lips twitch and refused to acknowledge that she'd slipped up. Maybe she did care that he hadn't bled to death, who wouldn't?

"I can see someone needs to bring levity back to this conversation," Jonas said with a note of resignation. "Do you remember the first time I flew back to Austin and you opened your front door wearing only that black lace bustier, matching panties and high heels?"

Alyx gasped in disbelief. "Excuse me! I still had on my skirt—and the vest, even though it was unbuttoned. That's why I wore a strapless bra, as I said at the time."

"Yeah, yeah, supposedly the air conditioner in the courthouse was acting up so you needed to be able to take off your jacket without straps sticking out."

"No 'supposedly' about it."

"But it was a bustier."

Exasperated, Alyx flung the bloody bandages into the trash basket, then scooped up the plastic lining and began tying it for disposal. "Fine. Do you know anything about designer clothes? You could donate two ribs and a kidney and not be able to button some of those vests. I needed the help."

"No, you didn't, but you looked fantastic—and I was only trying to tell you that it's my favorite memory of you…of us."

He looked and sounded so apologetic, that Alyx couldn't resist him, let alone keep to her stubborn resolve not to be amused by his version of the memory. "It was Halloween and you asked me if that was my trick-or-treat outfit."

"That's right, it was. I did."

"And you're saying that's your favorite memory? What about the drive back to town after E.D. and Dylan's wedding at the ranch?"

Dropping his head back, Jonas groaned up at the ceiling. "That was a memory? I thought that was one of my wet dreams between visits."

He was an incorrigible flirt. A smart woman would never believe a word he said, whether flattery or promises.

"You'd just climbed off my lap," he recalled, narrowing his eyes.

Yes, and resumed her seat on the passenger side just seconds before a state trooper drove past them. What a close call…and what scandal if the entire nightmare had played out. That was another reason they were better off having split up; he did bad things to her self-preservation instincts.

"Imagine Dylan getting that call for help minutes after leaving for their honeymoon," Jonas drawled.

No way, Alyx thought with a shake of her head. "I would have called *my* lawyer." No way would she put E.D. and Dylan—or herself for that matter—through such humiliation.

Jonas brushed her hair back from her face. "I like how your hair curls when you get all agitated and indignant."

Alyx tilted her head away. "I need to check on Grace and get rid of these bloody bandages."

Jonas plucked the bag out of her grasp. "I'll do that— and get the glasses to pour us another glass of wine."

"You've bled quite a bit, are you sure that's wise?"

"Your aversion to blood is making it worse than it is," he said gently.

"Maybe, but you'll have to drive, too."

"Not yet…unless you just gave me a not-so-subtle hint to leave?"

"No," she said without thinking. She quickly added, "What about flying tomorrow?"

"We're closed tomorrow, and so far we don't have any reservations for Monday." Taking hold of her chin, he forced her to meet his gaze. "So, now the truth—do I stay or do I go?"

Maybe she was being a fool, but losing herself in his eyes, Alyx couldn't help but nod. "I'd like it very much if you'd stay."

For an instant, Jonas looked as though he'd come back with something flip or flirtatious, but he simply lowered his head and touched his lips to hers. "Thank you. So would I."

Grace had recovered from her earlier scare and was ready to reign from her throne, the ottoman in the living room. Taking out her slices of chicken breast from the refrigerator to mix with dry dog food, Alyx focused on what to offer Jonas. He'd just returned with the wineglasses.

"What about dinner?" she asked him. "You probably should have something in your stomach as well as wine, especially if you need to take pain pills later tonight."

"I won't, but I will admit I'm getting hungry."

"Then why don't you lie down in the living room and I'll run to the market for a few things?"

"Don't do that. Anything you have here is fine."

Alyx gave him a wry look. "Well, you can't have Grace's chicken, and I think you need something more substantial than rabbit food."

"In that case, I'll come with you."

How sweet, he was worried that she would run into that big lug again. "I'm sure I'll be fine."

"We can always go to a restaurant."

He looked as enthusiastic about that as she did about the prospect of her yearly physical. Besides that, she didn't want this day to end the way they always had in the past— sex followed by polite, safe conversation while being hovered over by waiters. Like anyone who enjoyed good food, culture and ambiance, Alyx loved an excellent dinner out, but that wasn't what was needed tonight.

"You're in no shape for that. In fact, you'll probably raise eyebrows at the market, too, with all of your bandages. If you insist on coming, you're welcome, but I'd feel better if you stay put."

"Then grab a couple of TV dinners and be done with it."

Perplexed, Alyx collected her leather bag and drew out her compact to check for smudges and to redo her lipstick. "Are you worried that I'll give you food poisoning?"

"Of course not. But I can be really content with a burger and beer."

"I want food, not empty calories." Snapping the compact shut, Alyx nodded toward the living room. "Go chill before I change my mind."

An hour later, Jonas opened his eyes to realize that what had wakened him was the tempting aroma emerging from the kitchen. For a moment he remained still, meeting Grace's shy but curious gaze.

He stifled a yawn and told the dog, "That's for me. You already had yours." But as he sat up and eased himself to his feet, he did stroke her sleek back. "Thanks for the company, cutie."

Wandering into the kitchen, he found the appealing sight of Alyx wearing a full apron imprinted with a map of Italy that displayed the various wine regions on it. She looked delectable herself with her dark hair pulled back in a loose ponytail at her nape and tendrils curling around her face. As for the assortment of pots and pans and the aromas, he had no words.

"Am I about to learn that you're a Cordon Bleu chef?"

Alyx glanced up from the cutting board where she was chopping spinach. "Hardly. But ever since I had my own place—I mean after law school and everything—when the workload got progressively heavier, I discovered that it was soothing to me to spend time in the kitchen. It's not something I get to do often enough, but since I spend most of my holidays alone—"

"Do you?" Jonas searched his memory banks and came up short. "I thought your parents were still alive?"

"Why?" she asked with a sardonic glance. "Because I've injected them into my conversations so much?"

She'd been doing a good deal of thinking while at the market, Jonas concluded, and was planning to put space between them again. "No, wise guy, because you're so young."

The knife paused a second over the spinach before she went back to chopping. "You *are* a breath of fresh air. Sleep well?"

Grateful for her quick thinking in avoiding yet another clash, he toasted her with his glass—whether she noticed *that* or not. "I did. Thank you for strong-arming me. It looks like you've been busy. What are we having? It sure smells great."

"Spinach enchiladas."

"Mexican cuisine I've had. Spinach enchiladas…what's that, toss the cow and replace it with rabbit food?"

"It was adapted for vegetarians, but you can mix in meat or beans, use cheddar instead of Monterey Jack…it's delicious, Jonas. You won't be disappointed."

She spoke with such enthusiasm, he settled onto the nearest bar stool content to watch—and listen. "I'm sure it will be," he said. "Tell me more."

"About dinner?"

"Anything you want to share."

For a moment she pursed her lips. "For the record? My mother died five years ago in her sleep. I think after losing my brother, she lost heart—and whatever feelings she had for my father."

That one he hadn't expected. "She was very young."

"Barely fifty-six."

"Sad. That must have made things between you and your father all the more difficult. Do you keep in touch with him?"

With the slightest shake of her head, Alyx replied, "After a few awkward attempts, we both decided a break was needed."

"That's understandable. And now?"

"Status quo?" Alyx paused and stared at one of the backsplash tiles displaying a colorful array of chili peppers. "I think it's a lucky thing if we can recognize when it's healthier to stop ingesting poisonous relationships as though we're chain-smokers, or trying to mold people into our vision for them. Not everything can be cured with love, any more than it can be subdued through dominance—and who wants to be the caretakers of that swill if it happens?"

As soon as that tidy speech was delivered, Alyx glanced over her shoulder as though wondering, "Did I just say that?"

"It's the Alyx Carmel that first bowled me over in her office," he replied with an admiring smile. "You're a passionate woman. It's only natural that your opinions are, too."

She burst into laughter. "I know a few dozen people who would agree with that."

Jonas found that a rare and enjoyable sound. "You need to laugh more."

Carrying the pan to the island where he was sitting, she began to construct the enchiladas. "No doubt, but I'm not in the right business for being lighthearted." Taking a sip of her wine, she added, "What about your family? Who's left?"

"My son, Blake. He splits holidays between Claudia and me. Once school is in summer break, we try to spend two weeks together traveling."

"Camping?"

"No, Blake requires electrical access. He's not happy without his laptop and other gizmos."

"Did you get to do that this year? Where did you go?"

"Denver, then Salt Lake City. We'd done all of the coastal cities and decided to start on the interior of the country. Last year we did Chicago. I'm not sure how many more times we'll do that since next year we'll be sweating the driving issue—or rather I will. He's more than ready."

"What about your parents?"

"My father passed the first year after I graduated from the Academy. My mother remarried and lives in Connecticut."

"Happily I hope?"

"Seems to be."

"Last I heard, my father was between women."

Alyx spoke so casually, Jonas almost suspected her of attempting some dark humor. "Give me a minute to decide if that's disturbing or not."

"More likely it means women wise up faster these days. Once they realize what a catch he's *not,* they flee." Adding the grated cheese to the line of rolled tortillas, Alyx carried the glass pan to the oven and checked the temperature. "Did you ever tell me about any siblings?"

Jonas smiled. "You never asked."

"And you never offered information unless I did." She returned to the island and touched her glass to his. "So I'm asking."

"An older sister who lives near our mother and stepfather. That gives them two other grandkids—a boy and girl—so Blake isn't under too much pressure to visit." Rising, Jonas circled the island and took Alyx's glass from her hand and placed it on the granite counter. "Are we done with the small talk?" he asked, slipping his arms around her waist.

"Was that small talk? I thought you said we should share."

"So I did. Thank you for playing nice. Want to share this?" he murmured, lowering his head.

As he kissed her, he drew her fully against his body. It pleased him that she yielded and seemed so relaxed with him. She also tasted better than any food she might be preparing.

"Watch that arm," she said as he tightened his hold. "I picked up more gauze while at the market, but that doesn't mean I want to use it."

"Nag, nag," he whispered, only to gently nibble on her earlobe. "How much time before dinner is ready?"

"Not long enough for what you have in mind."

There was no point in denying he was aroused again. He couldn't be around her without that happening, and he wanted her to know how desirable she was to him. Groaning softly, he backed her to the counter and pressed himself into the juncture of her thighs.

"Are you going to let me spend the night?"

Alyx sighed. "Jonas, is that wise? You really need to be careful with that arm."

"What if I promised to let you be on top the next two times?"

"Oh, you're that fast a healer?"

"Okay, you convinced me—the next two days. See how flexible I can be?"

"I guess we'll find out," she murmured, sliding her hand between them.

The sweet torment had him closing his eyes, yet pressing himself against her palm. "Then again, you could hop up on this counter."

"Can't. There's just time enough to make a salad."

Swearing softly, Jonas said with some discomfort, "I hope you're not going to make dessert?"

"It's already ready."

"I didn't see anything."

"You're looking at her," Alyx replied, smiling.

Chapter Ten

How could this be happening to me? It had barely been twenty-four hours.

Ironically the satellite radio station on the TV started playing an old classic that was almost word-for-word her thoughts. She turned up the volume and began singing along and was halfway through the first stanza when the phone rang. She was closer to the phone than the remote and grabbed for it.

"Preston residence," she began.

"Alyx…what are you listening to?"

Parke's impatient query over the phone had Alyx hurrying to the TV to turn off the radio station included in her cousin's service package. "Nothing. I was reading your instructions for watering your indoor plants. I got sidetracked while switching through satellite radio stations. How are you?"

"I think I'm coming home."

The news sent Alyx doing a 360 in the kitchen. Unfortunately, there was nowhere to collapse in shock. She had to settle for leaning against the closest cabinet. "Now?"

"I wish. I'll e-mail you my flight information as soon as I make my final decision."

Alyx smoothed her hand over her hair, trying to follow her cousin's thinking. "Okay, fine. Are you going to tell me what's happened that's made you want to cut your trip so short? You aren't enjoying Italy? You said Corrado and Ilsa were great."

"I adore Italy and they're lovely. I couldn't ask for a more gracious host and hostess."

"Then what's wrong? You're not learning as much as you hoped to?"

"It's nothing like that. I could spend the rest of my life here and not absorb all there is to see and digest." After an anguished sigh, Parke blurted out, "Remember when I was stood up for lunch?"

"The almost-sixty art dealer. Who can forget, since you almost bit my head off for suggesting he was affair material."

"Yes, well, I owe you an apology because he's showed up since then and admitted the reason for his poor behavior. He wants me."

"To borrow from the younger generation, duh," Alyx drawled. However, since her cousin sounded truly miserable, Alyx continued more sympathetically, "At least he has good taste."

"Thank you, but I'm not in the mood to be amused."

"Ah, Parke. I know you're not attracted to him, but you have to be at least a little flattered. He's a successful and intelligent man, and as you said very connected."

"He's married—*and* has at least one lover on the side."

"Good grief! When would he have time to sell your work, let alone woo you? Tell him to take a hike." Alyx didn't grasp the problem. Why ruin an experience of a lifetime for some aging Casanova who wanted to put a few more notches in his belt before his equipment wore out?

"I couldn't do that."

"Why not? It's nothing less than he deserves."

"I mean, I can't because the attraction is mutual."

"Oh." *Oh!* Well, that did put a different spin on things. Alyx had been "in lust" with a married man once or twice herself. She'd never acted upon the impulses, but she could sympathize with women who did stumble upon those complex feelings. But she couldn't imagine being attracted to a man who was married *and* had a mistress; she was a little too proud for that much sharing. "My, my, my," she murmured to her cousin. "He must have some personality…or something."

"Please, Alyx," Parke groaned. "It's not like I asked for this."

"No, sweetie, you didn't. I suppose I should ask what running away will do? You want him to represent you there, don't you—or is that off the table now? If it isn't, then you'd have to speak with him from time to time."

"That's true, but at least there would be plenty of distance between us."

Alyx didn't know when she'd heard her cousin sound this concerned about her willpower. "It would also help to remind yourself that if he's willing to cheat on his lover, you're probably not the only other temptation he's salivating over."

"He swears there's only Eva and she would be his wife if divorce wasn't so difficult here."

Good grief, Alyx thought, shaking her head. "Do you hear yourself? It's easy enough for him to dismiss the first wife, claim he would want to be married to the second woman, and yet you're supposed to throw yourself into his arms? He's a cad—and I would be afraid to let him touch me for fear of what diseases I could be contracting."

"That's why I knew I needed to call you," Parke said dryly. "You always manage to shear away any romance from a situation with that sharp legal mind of yours and stick to the cold, hard facts."

Alyx winced, but knew better than to protest. Her unemotional approach to most things—with the exception of people she loved, like Parke and E.D. and the irrepressible G-man—was why she could bill three figures an hour and could be picky about the clients she wanted to work for. This was an instance when her cousin needed to hear the hard truth to get her away from a situation she would later regret. But the end of Parke's situation would definitely put an end to Alyx's complicated one.

Jonas had stayed the night, and Sunday, as well. It had been an unspoken experiment between them, as though neither wanted to jinx the delicate magic evolving by jeopardizing it with analysis. They'd shared a leisurely breakfast, walked and played with Grace, and had made love with a greater passion *and* tenderness than ever before. They'd been…like a couple falling in love.

"You want me to stay here, don't you?"

Jerked back from that revelation, Alyx pressed her hand to her aching diaphragm. "Good grief, Parke, of course not."

"Things are going well between you and Mystery Man, is that it?"

She wasn't about to respond to that, especially since Parke was so tortured herself. "This is your home. Make your arrangements and let me know when to pick you up. It's time I got back to reality anyway."

"Just because I'm coming home is no reason for you to run off."

"I'm not running." That didn't sound honest even to Alyx's ears. "I'm feeling good, great actually," she added more brightly. "I've lost just about all the weight I'd gained, the shoulder feels the best it has since I was wounded, and while there's no immediate urgency work-wise, it wouldn't hurt to get back and ease my way into my normal routine." Though how she was going to tell Jonas, she had no idea.

"You could stay the rest of the time I'd planned being away and we could visit while your guy is—did you tell me if he's on vacation, too, or working, or what?"

"His name is Jonas." She had to tell Parke at least that much.

"That's a nice strong name. What does he do?"

"He's helping a friend with his business. The friend broke his leg. It's complicated."

"Isn't everything anymore?"

"Yes." Maybe that was another reason to go home. She was feeling protective and possessive of her time with Jonas. She couldn't do that. Things were bound to change drastically whether he stayed with the Bureau or not.

"Alyx…I'm getting the sense that we should be talking about you more than me."

Heaven forbid. "Please just do what you feel you need

to do and let me know your flight schedule. I'll let Shar know that you'll be resuming your regular hours at the spa sooner than anticipated also."

"Well, give me tonight to think about it."

"What's there to think about? You're an American, Parke, and you're considering entering a harem—hello!"

Her cousin burst into laughter. "Thank you. There went the rest of my romantic fantasies."

Alyx frowned at her scuffed sneakers. Is that what she'd done? "There's nothing wrong with romance. It's who you share it with that matters."

"Right again. I suspect he would drain me dry. I could never fly to Europe enough to suit him. He's already made it clear that he doesn't like to fly so it would all be on me to reconnect and with my work selling as well as it is, that would cut into my creativity. That doesn't feel like a good idea, let alone a fair proposition."

"For a couple who haven't had sex yet, you two have been doing a serious amount of talking."

"You're telling me."

"Just out of curiosity, would he be paying for your tickets to come see him?"

Parke's muted utterance sounded like a GI facing yet another hypodermic needle upon arrival at boot camp. "I honestly don't know."

Alyx disliked the guy more and more with every insight her cousin shared. Glancing at the stove clock and knowing the international minutes were costing her cousin plenty, she sought to give her a reprieve from these painful admissions. "You'd better sleep on this, Parke, and call me tomorrow."

"You're disappointed in me, aren't you?"

"Heavens, no." Alyx sighed. "Maybe I'm a bit confused that you can feel what you do knowing how he's so clearly manipulating you. This is not the independent and sure-minded Parke Preston whose work receives raves for its boldness and daring as much as for its beauty."

"It must be this gorgeous country casting a spell on me."

"It's equally magnificent here, Parke, in its own way. A man doesn't change that."

"Jeez, you're worse than an MRI machine. So maybe I'm realizing I don't want to solo it the rest of my life without someone to love. I'm not even talking marriage, necessarily, but it's not a bad thing to admit you're lonely."

"No, but you don't have to give up most of who you are for that, either. What's next, your self-respect?"

"I was beginning to think maybe I had too much of that," Parke said. "Pride, I mean."

"Let's make a pact, okay?" Swallowing at the sudden lump in her throat, Alyx continued, "I'll tell you when you get too incorrigible for anyone to love, and you come home so I can get back to Austin and slay rotten spouses like your would-be lover via the courts."

With a reluctant chuckle, Parke said, "Okay, I'll call you."

Jonas had to try dialing three times to get through to Alyx. "You okay?" he asked when he finally heard her voice.

"Did you try to call? Sorry, I was on the phone with Parke."

"The only acceptable excuse. How are things in Italy?"

"She's coming home."

Jonas had been driving to the airport and pulled over to the side of the road. It didn't take a Ph.D. to figure out that the physics of their relationship was about to undergo an extreme 180-degree turn. Of all the lousy timing. "When?" he asked, hoping he sounded calmer than he felt. He felt…his heart had slammed so hard against his sternum that he could almost believe he'd suffered a fracture.

"She says she'll call me tomorrow to tell me her flight schedule."

"Is something wrong?" He hated asking, partly out of dread of what he would hear and partly because he was talking way too much; he needed her to provide information. But when she remained silent, he had no choice but to prod. "Alyx? Did something happen over there? I hear it's a fantastic country, but in this day and age, travel just about anywhere can be dangerous for Americans."

"In more ways than one," she replied wryly.

Raising his eyebrows, Jonas said, "That sounds provocative."

"This is about a man, Jonas. Many southern women remain under the conviction that they're incomplete without a man, and while Parke may be more feminist than most of them, she's still got the gene, buried as she tries to keep it."

He didn't know if he was supposed to laugh or wire magnolias in sympathy. From the photos he'd spotted in the house, he'd concluded that, like Alyx, Parke was a stunner, so there was no escaping the obvious question, "What's the problem with the man? And before you answer that, it wouldn't hurt to remember what kind of phone I'm on."

"Then let's just say that she received an offer that she can't accept."

Rubbing his face for what that could suggest, Jonas hoped he was wrong in his first guess. He didn't want to consider what HQ would do if they found out that he was involved with someone whose family had connections to organized crime figures.

"Are you there?"

"I'm trying not to stick my foot all the way down my throat. Alyx, you're not saying what I think you're saying?"

"Well, now you have me wondering what you *think* I'm saying."

"'Make her an offer she can't accept'? What besides the obvious am I supposed to surmise from that?"

"Oh. No-no! At least she hasn't mentioned the need to 'go to the mattresses.' Although, considering the way he's setting up the rules for her, maybe it's a possibility."

"And I'm beginning to think this conversation needs to wait until this afternoon unless you can come up to the airport." Even as he suggested that, Jonas knew she'd decline. She wasn't about to expose herself to Miranda, and he couldn't blame her.

"I'd better stay here in case Parke calls again. She sounds as distraught as I've ever heard her. Jonas, the man in question is almost twice her age…and he already has one lover besides his wife."

"Is that the problem? She's concerned about a little competition?"

"What kind of perspective is that?"

"When you find out what vitamins he's taking, let me know."

"That's not funny. Let's see how many wisecracks you make when I return to Austin without saying goodbye."

Her indignant tone had Jonas glancing at the clock and then his BlackBerry for the day's appointment schedule thus far. If nothing else showed up, he could be in her driveway in two hours…unless he could beg mechanical problems and cancel the other two reservations he had this afternoon. No, of course he couldn't. So that left back-pedaling and apology as his options.

"Alyx. Take a deep breath and give me a chance to explain."

"Oh, no need," she replied with a mirthless laugh. "You were perfectly clear in what you meant. You tell me that you want me to be more open with you and share my feelings and concerns, then the moment I am—"

"Stop." Jonas knew he was risking everything, but if they couldn't mend this trivial breach, then he had to accept they just didn't speak the same language. "I want you to feel free to share, yes. But how crazy is this?" As soon as the words were out, he regretted them and added what was his core concern, "You can't be leaving yet."

"It's inevitable. She's looking at what's available flight-wise and how big the penalty they'll charge her for the switch."

"Why does that mean you have to go home?"

"Because I won't be needed anymore. She's an artist. She'll come home emotionally wrung out and wound up and probably want to lose herself in her work. She keeps weirder hours than I do. Or she'll just want privacy. Any way you look at it, I'll be in the way." Pausing, Alyx took a deep breath and added, "Jonas, forgive me for my rude reaction. I'm still stunned at what Parke was actually considering, as much as at learning my time here would be cut short, but that's no excuse. I'd love for you to come by later, if and when you're free."

* * *

He was there before Venus could be seen descending behind the grand red monuments for the last time that season. For the rest of the year the planet of love would be the morning star for early risers. Jonas wondered if that was good luck or not? He knew he needed all the luck he could get and he wasn't about to dis a goddess, as the kids said.

Something had to be working in his favor—as he strode up the sidewalk, she opened the front door. Before she could finish explaining that Grace had heard his arrival and informed her, he swept her into his arms.

"I was beginning to believe someone had asked for a sunset flight," she began. Then she couldn't say more because he'd silenced her with an impassioned kiss.

While he was far from rough, Jonas made it clear how eager he'd been to get here and how good it felt to hold her against him. "Thank goodness no one did," he said. "I'd have been forced into buying them off if it meant not getting to see you before you leave."

"Jonas, Parke hasn't called again. She may have changed her mind."

"Something tells me that she won't—which, for the record, professionally and as a man who believes in the whole one-man-one-woman thing, is my idea of sound judgment."

"Yes, I would have told her that from the instant the man started his sales pitch."

Then Alyx had ten times the smarts of her cousin, regardless of Parke's talent. "So we need to talk," he murmured, although from the way he held her it was clear he had something else in mind first.

She hid her face against his shoulder. "Yes. But please not tonight. Could we hold off until tomorrow over coffee?"

Jonas lifted his head and tightened his arms. "Are you saying you want me to stay?" He all but held his breath waiting for her to decide.

"I hope you can and will."

Jonas released her only to pet a waiting Grace and close the door. "Sweetheart, there's nowhere else I'd rather be."

For hours he'd worried that what ground they'd recovered in the last several days was lost. That had put serious cracks in his confidence. But Alyx's eager embrace soon had him forgetting that injury. Kissing Alyx, Jonas realized, would forever be his connection to dreams of what could be.

"Can I get you a glass of wine?" she asked him.

"I'm high enough just looking at you."

If Alyx had shown reluctance at any instance, he would have backed off but, in fact, she smiled and held him with the same fervor. Deciding that unless Grace sank her teeth into his calf, he had plans. Jonas swung Alyx up into his arms and carried her to the guest bedroom that she'd made hers and laid her across the bed.

"You look too perfect to touch," he said, giving her a last chance to bolt. She was lovely in her white satin robe, her dark hair cascading around her like a dark pool.

"I hope that doesn't stop you," she murmured, drawing him down to her.

Thus began an evening Jonas suspected would be forever burned in his memory. He'd thought he knew about lovemaking; Alyx taught him a new dimension.

He'd never felt more peace and yet more need than when

lying against her, inhaling her scent. The only thing better would be to feel them naked together and he wasted no time in making that a reality. Alyx had prepared for him with her minimal attire, only the robe and her best lace panties beneath. Knowing she'd dressed for him, had been preparing for him, only added to his hunger. He rose only long enough to strip, while she turned down the crisp sheets.

She moved like a caress of sun-warmed air flowing over the mesa, bringing him to life and filling him with hope and resilience. Jonas wanted to praise her, thank her, but the words were trapped, building in his chest like the hunger building in his groin. Hoping she didn't mind his lack of patience, he urged her back onto the bed and brushed her robe off her shoulders to adore her with his mouth.

To his surprise, she stiffened. Although his move had been subtle, he had to ask, "Did I hurt you?"

"No, I must have set the air conditioner too low, that's all. Would you mind if I slip my arms back into my robe?"

She wasn't cold, Jonas knew. Steam all but emanated from her. Then it struck him—it wasn't as dark as she would probably have liked it to be, and inevitably her mind was on her scars and what he would remember if she did have to say goodbye to him.

"Put your arms around me." He spread kisses up her stomach and over each breast. When he reached her lips, he slid into her slowly. "I'll keep you warm. In sunshine or moonlight, you never have to feel shy or hide from me, don't you know that by now? I adore your body as much as I'm in awe of your courage, but do you think if you ran from me tomorrow, those scars are what I'd visualize?" His breath hitched slightly as he drew out and entered her again. "Uh-uh. I'd be seeing your expression as it is now with your lips moist from my kiss, your eyes glowing from the feel of me inside you, your hands biting into my hips because you want more of me."

A strange expression came over her face and Jonas knew that whatever endearments he told her now—or for that matter had told her the last time they'd made love—were just words to her. Damage was damage and you couldn't erase it with willpower or verbal compliments. Only time and proving his unfailing delight in her might remove the worst memories and doubt. He had to fight for that opportunity.

Brushing his lips along her collarbone, his teeth along the graceful length of her neck, he rasped, "All right, then believe in this."

He stroked her with the earned intimacy of a longtime lover, probing with his fingers where they were joined just to feel her spasm and arch closer. He cupped and caressed each full and taut breast, teasing her with his tongue and teeth. Listening to her soft yearning sounds, Jonas urged her to ecstasy, and when she cried out her climax, he locked his mouth to hers and drove to his own release.

Alyx wasn't a snuggling type of woman. She'd fought too hard for her independence, and her profession had made her even less inclined to be clingy. However, after the first waves of passion ebbed, instead of rolling onto her back and, sated, stretching her arms overhead to hug her pillow, she let Jonas keep her lying across his chest, and listened to the reassurance of his strong heartbeat.

"Not cold anymore?" Jonas murmured.

She had a good mind to pinch him where the mark wouldn't show, but decided he'd been too wonderful to deserve that. It had surprised her, too, that she'd had a sudden case of self-consciousness, until she started focusing on him rather than on herself. With a contented sigh, she combed her fingers through his chest hair. "I've decided this is the second most tantalizing thing next to your kisses," she replied.

"Do tell?" He stroked her from shoulder to hip and left his hand there. "Should other parts of the anatomy feel left out and have hurt feelings?"

Alyx grinned. "Absolutely not. You're an entirely gorgeous man. From our first time together, I literally had to force myself to leave you and open a briefcase full of affidavits and disclosure briefs."

"Why, counselor, that's a compliment to treasure." He stroked her hair. "I told you we fitted."

"Mmm. What do your friend and his wife think of you suddenly abandoning their home?"

"The truth is, having me under their roof was a necessary evil. If they knew who or where you are, they'd be trying to drug *you* with magnolias as insurance to keep me here."

Alyx laughed out loud at the southern charm reference. "I've been vaccinated."

"That's probably a good thing. If you were a full-fledged magnolia you'd be lethal."

Alyx glanced up at him and tapped him on the heart. "You did fall for a Yankee version of Scarlett once."

"Full disclosure—Claudia's people were originally from *Olde* Virginia. I guess you could say that I've been vaccinated, too."

"Good grief, we have more in common than I thought!"

Jonas's gaze heated and he rubbed his thumb over her lower lip, still swollen from his kisses. "I bet we do. Favorite place to be kissed?"

Alyx nuzzled the nipple nearest her mouth. "Too easy. You've been there and you've done that."

"I was giving you a chance to start your Santa list early."

"Ho-ho!" Intrigued with the question, she lifted her head to meet his wicked smile. "Favorite spectator sport?"

"Strip poker."

"That isn't a spectator sport," she scoffed.

"It is if you keep winning."

Alyx might have been amused if she didn't immediately think about who he might like to watch lose her clothes. The spasm of jealousy she suffered was anything but pleasant and she rolled off him to lie back on her pillow.

Jonas followed, resting his head on his hand. He lazily ran his other hand in a serpentine path from the hollow of her throat to her knee. "That was an extremely interesting reaction."

"Enjoy it while it lasts."

"I am." As her nipple responded to his caresses, he lowered his head to wet it then graze her gently with his teeth.

"Wretch."

"So what would you have said?"

"Never mind, it would have been boring."

"Trust me," he murmured, initiating the serpentine caress again. "I'm anything but bored. Favorite spectator sport?"

"The truth? It's a toss-up between figure skating and

ballroom dancing. I don't get to see much grace or eloquence of expression in my work—creative anger, yes. Anyway, it strikes me that both skills need exceptional discipline, and let's face it, the participants are mostly *young* people. I often find myself thinking if we could transfer that dedication to relationships, we'd have fewer divorces."

Jonas took hold of her hand and raised it to his lips. "That's a profound observation. You see a great deal of sadness, not just the ugliness in people, don't you?"

She'd been aware of his returning arousal for several moments and reaching down to stroke him, she purred, "That's why I like to observe and surround myself with beautiful things, haven't you noticed?"

"As a matter of fact, I have." Closing his hand around hers to tighten her hold, he replied, "You'd be a knockout in any of those costumes. Favorite dance?"

"This one," she said, offering her mouth as she shifted to welcome him into her body.

Listening to Jonas murmur his pleasure, Alyx eased him onto his back, then covered him with her body. Cupping her bottom with his hands, he thrust himself fully into her moist heat, just as she found the same inviting and tantalizing home in his mouth. Their strokes were slow and restrained, as disciplined and thorough as a skilled dancer honoring the tempo of the music that hummed in their veins.

When she would have sat up, though, Jonas kept her locked against him. "Stay with me like this," he whispered. "I want to feel all of you."

Alyx's hair became a veil of privacy for their erotic kisses. They built to a sweet torture, dragging soft moans from each other, and their bodies grew slick, making each caress and thrust more provocative. If they ever did dance together, she wouldn't be able to stop remembering this sensual tango.

Just when she thought she would be torn in half from heart to womb from the intense yearning, Jonas rolled her onto her back and, twining his fingers between hers, he stared down at her with rapt concentration and surged into her again.

"Tell me it's never been like this with anyone else?" he demanded.

"You know that."

"And it never will," he muttered and surged again, then again until she couldn't help but cry out.

To Alyx, he seemed almost angry. Gone was the take-everything-with-a-grain-of-salt playboy who enjoyed sensual romps, but kept his deepest inner feelings to himself. Here was a different Jonas Hunter with emotions naked and feelings raw. Did he resent her for reaching this depth in him? Was he so ingrained with the Bureau life, that he had lost touch with his soul?

Her heart all but broke for that, for him. She'd never felt such anguish and tenderness in her life. "Jonas, darling... I'm yours," she whispered urgently. "For as long as you want me."

"I'll go to my grave wanting you."

With that thickly groaned confession, he crushed his mouth to hers and raced them to a shattering climax.

So this was what it was like. Alyx's pounding heart felt almost too large for her chest, and she had the strongest urge to burst into tears. Gently extricating her hands from his, she wrapped her arms around him and stroked his back and the damp hair at his nape.

"Jonas, don't be angry because you feel or want more than you thought you did."

He went absolutely still, even stopped breathing for an instant and all that moved was his heart pounding even more fiercely than hers. Slowly lifting his head, he uttered, "I don't just want you." Drawing a shaky breath, he added gruffly, "I love you."

Like a snowball subjected to a microwave oven, Alyx totally melted. "Well, you don't look very happy about it."

"You wouldn't either if you found yourself totally nuts about someone who saw you as little more than a sex toy. A favorite one—probably only admitted under duress—but merely entertainment nonetheless."

"Oh, you have it all figured out, do you?"

Once again he went still. Then he reached over and turned on the bedside light. Looming over her, he studied her face with all of the seriousness of an interrogator. Slowly his expression went from grim to wondrous and tender. Gently, he caressed her cheek.

"Help me out here, counselor. I'm feeling uniquely obtuse."

"It's a bit of a revelation to me, as well," she replied wryly.

When she didn't blurt out the admission as he had, he growled, "Damn it, Alyx, say it."

"I love you, too."

In the end that alone couldn't change anything, she realized. In fact, it would now make things all the more complicated, which would add to their problems, but for this moment, she let herself bask in the honeyed glow of rapture, perfectly culminating in Jonas's passionate embrace and possessive kiss. She loved and was a beloved.

Miracles do happen, she thought, even when you're not looking for them.

"How long have you known?" he demanded.

"It had to have been coming on gradually, but I was certain just now when I saw how upset you seemed to be—and that hurt. 'Love doesn't wound,' isn't that the way it's written?" Then curiosity got the best of her. "When did it hit you?"

"When I saw you again at the market." His expression grew dark with fury and he winced as though feeling an unexpected stab. "And then to see that no-good creep put his hands on you…he's lucky I didn't tear out his arm."

"My bloodthirsty hero."

Jonas chuckled, only to grow sober and kiss her with breathtaking gentleness. "Thank you. I'd about resigned myself to having to settle for your lust."

"Don't undersell it. Lust matters a great deal," she said, stroking her fingers through his chest curls again.

"Especially now," he murmured against her lips.

Of course, they made love again, and this time they left the lights on.

Chapter Eleven

"What if I moved to Texas?"

If Alyx thought Parke's announcement yesterday had shocked her, Jonas's had her choking on her first sip of coffee the next morning. She burned her tongue, too, but managed not to destroy the section of the newspaper that he'd picked up to read.

"What do you mean?" she croaked between coughs.

His expression went from concern for her to wounded. "What kind of response was that?"

"About as honest as I can get." Rising from the barstool at the counter, Alyx ripped off a paper towel from the roller under a cabinet and returned to mop up the splashes of coffee. She knew Jonas was watching her with those keen, pale eyes, trying to read more of what she thought, and it was all she could do to keep her hands from trembling as she tried a second sip of coffee.

"So what was last night?"

She wasn't fooled by his casual tone; her reaction had disappointed him. But he was moving so fast. "How can that be an option right now—or were you considering asking to transfer to the Dallas or Houston offices?" They hadn't discussed the failed promotion again, but it appeared that couldn't be avoided, and she couldn't imagine him asking to transfer there and work under the person who'd been put ahead of him. She'd seen Jonas operate as an agent and knew he was a consummate professional, but he had his pride.

Jonas frowned and put down his own mug. "What would be the sense in that if you're in Austin? I simply assumed you wanted to see more of me."

"Of course, but—so you *have* decided to leave the Bureau?" She was careful not to use the word *quit.* "Is that wise without having a new position to move into?"

"Don't worry that I'd ask or expect you to support me."

"Jonas, I wasn't thinking that."

"I just thought—damn."

At night he left his cell phone on vibrate and right now it was jiggling like a kid's windup toy scrambling across the soapstone counter. Snatching it up, he flipped it on. "Yeah?" he growled.

There was a pause, then, "Sorry if this is bad timing. Do you recognize my voice?"

Jonas stiffened. "Sure."

"There's a situation and I need help. It's as bad as it gets. Not for me or us, but someone I care about. Can you come? Please be careful how you answer that."

Without emotion Jonas replied, "I have to get back to you on my other phone. Ten minutes. No more."

"Thank you."

He snapped the phone shut and met Alyx's worried and curious gaze. "I have to go."

"It sounds like it." From the distant expression in his eyes, he'd already left a minute ago. Something was wrong. "Is it the airport? What happened?"

"I really have to go." He snatched his keys and BlackBerry off the end of the counter. "I may be out of touch for a while."

"Yes…okay." Already dazed by what had transpired between them before the call, Alyx was slow to follow. "So I'll call you later to see about dinner?"

"Alyx, don't call me. I'll be in touch as soon as I can."

What on earth…? "Jonas, please. Don't leave like this. If this is about something I said—"

He strode back to her, gripped her by her upper arms and kissed her hard. "I love you."

And then he was gone.

Jonas drove midway between Alyx's and Zane's house before he pulled over and dug out the prepaid cell phone he had in the glove compartment of the Mustang. Referring to his BlackBerry, he punched in the fourth number in its address book. Before the first ring was completed, he had a connection.

"It's me," he said without waiting for a "hello."

"I really hate to put you on the spot. I know you're already committed where you are. I'm also going to have to tell you the worst of it straight off—you can't call this in to your people."

He was referring to the FBI, and Jonas immediately knew this was going to be worse than he feared. His throat was fire-torch dry; he was aware that Judge Dylan Justiss wouldn't be this cautious and demanding if it weren't critical. What he wanted to hear was that this wasn't about E.D. or their kids. "You called me, you know what you're getting," he said, shorthanding through the finer details. "What have you got?"

"Kidnapping. Boy, seven years old."

Jonas looked at the stratus clouds still blocking the sun. Although veil-thin, they lent a coolness to the morning, but would be burning off by the time he was supposed to fly. However, something told him that he wouldn't be flying today—at least not any of Zane's planes. "Why didn't the family call for an immediate Amber Alert?"

"Because the father's not your usual citizen. He's a billionaire, one of the increasingly numerous ones who made their fortune in technology-related areas, and he believed if he and his family kept a low-key life, they wouldn't be targeted by opportunists."

Recently—and after the fact—the Bureau had dealt with a home invasion for another billionaire, equally eccentric and naive. Fortunately for everyone involved, they'd all come out of it alive. Victims weren't always so lucky. "How long since the snatch?"

"Four hours."

Jonas grimaced. "Ransom call?"

"One hour ago."

Jonas rubbed at his forehead hard enough to take off skin, but he kept his tone flat not to attract any attention. One could never discount accidental reception. Since he wasn't targeted surveillance, he was fairly certain Big Brother wasn't listening. Still, Dylan had to know what he was asking. If this situation spiraled out of control and tanked, he wouldn't have to lose any more sleep over decisions about his future.

Then Alyx's lovely face flashed before his eyes.

"I'll say this again—this needs to be called in."

Dylan's voice dropped to barely audible. "And I'm telling you he won't do it. They convinced him that his son will be sacrificed if he pulls anything. From what I can gather, the kidnappers are willing to cut their losses and run, but they're not going to take any chances of being identified. I can't blame him, his son's bloody T-shirt was found stuffed in their morning newspaper. You should also know the boy is a hemophiliac."

Could it get worse? Silently swearing, Jonas started considering possibilities. Chances are the kidnappers knew of the boy's condition and were playing it to their advantage. A package of fresh hamburger meat could be useful to fool terrified parents long enough to make a lab sample a moot point. That would mean an insider was involved, a servant or employee. If it was an outsider who was aware of the family's wealth, but not the details of the boy's health, and he'd gotten the blood from the kid, things could already be out of control.

But there was a major hurdle even before he worried about that worst-case scenario.

"Two things you need to know," he said to Dylan before making his decision. "First, I'm not just on vacation to help a friend. I'm on leave. Self-directed due to a promotion that didn't come through."

A dejected sigh came over the air. "I don't know what to say."

"The point is that if this matter could be quickly resolved, I could cover my butt by claiming it was a situation I fell into and a judgment call was necessary. But regardless of whether this drags on or not," Jonas added, "the second problem is that you know it'll take me a couple of hours to reach the international airport where I can catch the next flight out. Am I really your best option when every minute matters?"

"I wish you'd trusted me enough to tell me this when we last talked," Dylan muttered.

"Yeah, like I wanted to share that happy news. Besides, I'd just run into a certain someone, remember?"

"She can't know about this. Not even my certain someone does."

"If you think I said anything other than goodbye," Jonas replied with equal warning, "you called the wrong number."

Dylan cleared his throat and said determinedly, "As far as I'm concerned, you're the best. That's why the person on whose behalf I'm calling has a private jet headed in your direction. It's due at your regional airport in just over an hour and the pilot knows to break speed records getting back here."

This wasn't the time for smiles, but Jonas couldn't resist replying dryly, "Pretty sure of yourself." But his mind continued to race.

This already had the bad vibrations of a catastrophe in the making. However, a little, undoubtedly terrified kid was in the hands of strangers who could be anything from thugs looking for a shortcut to prosperity to pedophiles to terrorists wanting to bankroll a plot and at the same time take out a capitalist big shot. Jonas felt he had no choice but to restart the Mustang.

"I'd better get off this line and go explain why I can't give two weeks' notice to my temporary employer," he told Dylan.

"Is he going to take a financial hit because of my asking you to break your word to him?"

This was why Jonas was willing to risk a great deal, perhaps everything. Dylan understood the debt involved in asking for favors.

"We can discuss that later," Jonas replied.

"Come knowing that no matter what happens, he'll be taken care of."

Jonas disconnected because there was nothing more that needed to be said.

"I can't get a flight out until tomorrow," Parke announced to Alyx.

Her cousin's call had come only minutes after Jonas left, and Alyx had to struggle to stay focused on what her cousin was saying, even though she was glad Parke had made the decision to remove herself from temptation. She planned to do the same thing. "At least you don't have to rush packing," she replied, reaching for the pad and pen next to the phone. "Give me the flight information. I'll book my own flight as soon as we hang up."

"You're not serious? Alyx, there's no need for you to rush off."

"It makes the most sense," Alyx assured her. "This way I deliver your SUV and, while you have to drive yourself, jet lag and all, at least you don't have to worry about driving me back to Albuquerque in a few days. I know Grace will be glad to have her lady home. I'm afraid I haven't given her quite the attention she's been wanting."

"We could visit and you could explain why not," Parke teased.

"Oh, you'll probably come home ready to get to work. I don't want to be in the way."

"There's always a chance that you can't get the flight you want tomorrow. I know how you loathe multiple layovers."

"Then I'll get a room at the airport hotel until I do manage a flight with only a Dallas or a Houston stop. Really, I hate the thought of your driving hundreds of miles through all of that empty country."

"I love you, too, but—" Parke uttered a sound of distress and frustration "—what's going on? You don't sound like yourself. And what about Mystery Man? Surely Jonas would be thrilled if you can stay longer?"

Alyx covered the mouthpiece of the phone just in time to keep Parke from hearing an irrepressible, ragged sob. "Maybe not," she finally managed.

"More mystery," Parke muttered. "Don't tell me that you two have had a lovers' spat already?"

"There was hardly time for that. He's gone."

It was midafternoon when the sleek logo-free corporate plane landed in Austin. By then Jonas had spoken to Dylan again, who'd introduced him to Harold Arthur Freeman, young John Samuel Freeman's father, and taken copious notes detailing everything about the abduction of "Jimbo," as the family affectionately called him, the house and neighborhood where they lived, their schedule and services they used.

H, as he preferred to be called, was the soft-spoken genius behind Digit Dynamics, a communications technology company that was key in shooting the science of images and data into a new realm. He employed 117 people in offices located not far from the University of Texas, a three-story building wisely identified by only its street number, 313. Security was twenty-four hours, but began at the door. There were no gates into the parking lot and cameras were only situated at the building's two entry-exits and at the elevators.

Equally disturbing was that while H had a state-of-the-art fire-alarm system and sprinklers built into his thirty-five-hundred-square-foot, two-story home, he had no alarm system, save his five-year-old daughter Faith's spoiled Chihuahua, Truffles. A widowed live-in housekeeper named Loretta had been with the family for three years and the children treated her like their grandmother. All other services were contract—the yard service, pool service, handyman needs. Sarah, H's wife, drove the children to school herself and then often spent her time doing volunteer work and choosing charities and foundations with which to share their wealth. Jonas concluded they were unassuming and private people who were living well under the radar of what they could afford, and foolishly believed that somehow protected them from predators of all kinds. Unfortunately, the world was full of those living in denial.

As he descended the plane's retractable stairs, he saw Dylan pull up in his black Navigator. The man sitting in the backseat, he concluded, was H. Jonas shook his head, having told Dylan that he'd done plenty and to back off now and return to his family. H was to come alone to pick him up. He should have suspected his friend wouldn't listen.

"Stubborn fool," he said as he climbed into the passenger seat and deposited his leather carry-on bag on the floorboard. Although he gripped Dylan's hand with affection for their long friendship, he also glared into the dark-eyed, noble face of the respected judge, who didn't look very judgelike in his short-sleeved denim shirt, jeans and boots. "Tell me that you at least kept an eye out for someone shadowing you?"

"I know the drill," Dylan replied, unflinching. "I also had H lie down back there until we entered the airport. And E.D. and the kids are at the ranch under Chris's watchful eye. They think we're going to have a little family time before school starts next week."

Chris Coats was the caretaker-foreman of Justiss's property outside of town. That appeased Jonas, but only somewhat. "So what is E.D. going to say if you don't show up for dinner tonight?"

"I'll deal with that when and if I have to," Dylan replied.

Jonas turned to the gaunt-faced man sitting in the back and extended his hand. "Mr. Freeman, Jonas Hunter. I'm sorry we have to meet under these circumstances."

With a gray cast to his skin and his hazel eyes reddened behind wire-rimmed glasses, H looked closer to sixty than forty-five, which was understandable under these circumstances. He was a slender man who clearly didn't live to eat, rather ate to live, and his blue-striped, short-sleeved shirt and khaki pants hung on him, also indicating he wasn't much into sports or exercise despite having told Jonas that they had a pool in back of his house.

"Thank you," H murmured. "My wife and I are very grateful that you're risking so much on our behalf."

Jonas shot Dylan a look that seethed. "Big mouth," he muttered, and dove straight into business. "Has there been any other contact or messages?"

"No. It's been eerily silent. As I told you earlier, we're to put five cashier's checks totaling a quarter-million dollars and made out to Cash in a lockable plastic bag. Then I'm to go to a designated mall fast-food counter and get an empty fast-food drink cup and lid. He told me to put the bag into the cup, and drop it in the trash can at the entry to the restrooms beside the food court. Then I'm to leave. I would find my son standing by my car waiting for me."

"What kidnapper demands cashier's checks?" Dylan asked.

"Could be someone who suspects cash would be marked or contain dye. There is some ingenuity to his thinking that way. Any bank would raise eyebrows at being asked to put all $250,000 in a cashier's check not made out to someone specific. This way Mr. Freeman can say that he intends to make a few anonymous donations."

"Okay," Dylan said. "But playing devil's advocate, what then do they do with the checks? Once they release Jimbo, they have to know all banks will be alerted to be on the lookout for them to show up as deposits."

"Maybe they think they'll be safe if they go to Oklahoma or Louisiana…or into Mexico."

H leaned forward. "If they just give us our son back, I would swear never to put out an alert."

Even if he weren't a father himself, Jonas's heart couldn't help but wrench at the anguish he heard in the man's voice. But his logic was dangerously flawed. "You do that, sir, and you not only open yourself up to a repeat incident like this, you also embolden the kidnappers to try this again on some other poor family." One glance at the suffering man, though, told Jonas that he wasn't able yet to feel concern for anyone but his boy, and he prompted kindly, "Tell me again about the man who called?"

"As I said, the voice was muffled as if he was covering the mouthpiece or something. Uh…and he spoke in a deeper monotone."

Jonas already had drawn his own conclusion, but asked, "Old? Young?"

"I'm not a good judge of things like that. The first time I heard my wife on the phone I thought she was a little girl."

"How was his English? Did he have an accent? Twang? Drawl?"

If anything, H looked thoroughly lost. "I don't even know I have an accent until I leave Texas. Let me think…he said 'gonna' instead of 'going to,' and addressed me as 'man.' When he said the name of the mall, I had to ask him where that was and he asked me if I was stupid. There was something different about how he dragged out *man* and *stupid*. I had to explain that I don't shop."

Jonas was intrigued. "He didn't accuse you of keeping him on the line so the police could trace him?"

"No."

"Then he's been watching to see if you follow directions and knows you haven't brought anyone in yet. Either that or he's bugged your phone, which somehow I doubt, but we'll need to check anyway. You're sure no one followed you to where Dylan had you park your car and picked you up?"

"Frankly, Agent Hunter, I was so shaken, I was lucky not to get pulled over by the police for erratic driving."

That wasn't heartening news. Jonas glanced at Dylan's profile. "What about you? I know you were watching."

"He turned into the strip mall parking lot alone and when we left in this car, no one followed us."

That could mean the guy was a rank amateur and this was his first snatch. Maybe he was even working alone, although somehow Jonas doubted it. It would be tough to keep tabs on a terrified little kid and tag after the money man.

"Please," he added to H, "make that Jonas. We don't need you addressing me that way in front of other people unless I want to ID myself."

H looked confused. "Who would that be? There's only Sarah, Faith and Loretta at the house."

"Your service people? Who takes care of the pool and yard?"

"Oh, I see what you mean. I'm not sure." He was getting increasingly befuddled and spoke as though in a dream. "You'll have to ask Sarah or Loretta to give you their schedules. But I understand, yes...Jonas."

Poor guy was a real geek who got lost in the details of his tech dreaming. Wife Sarah probably had to stop him from walking out the door in the morning without his shoes on. No wonder he hadn't realized how vulnerable he was.

Moving on to their next potential problem, he asked, "What excuse did you give your people at the office for not coming in?"

Nodding, H said with some relief, "Sarah thought of that. She called my secretary and told her that I'd contracted a stomach virus and would be out for the day."

"Good. Let's hope the secretary doesn't have a problem she needs answered and calls while you're not there."

"She might. Sometimes I do work at home."

Good Lord, the guy wasn't making things easy on him. Fighting his own frustration, Jonas asked, "Do you also let your son go out by himself and retrieve the newspaper at the end of your driveway?"

The thin-faced man blanched. "He…we were trying to teach him about chores and responsibility. Some kids at school were taunting him about not having the latest video game like they did, and we were telling him that he couldn't have every new thing just because other kids did, but that he could earn money to buy it himself."

"And no one saw a vehicle pull up and snatch him, yank off his T-shirt, and stick it and the note telling you not to call the police in the newspaper bag?" He didn't even get on the man about touching anything and ruining potential fingerprints or other DNA. If that had been Blake's T-shirt, he would have been hard-pressed to follow procedure.

H bowed his head. "I didn't even hear the fast acceleration as they drove off. Sarah did and she called Jimbo and then me, once she saw the front door was open. Ours is a quiet neighborhood of busy professional people, and the shrubbery up front pretty much blocks the view of the circular part of the driveway."

Jonas had dealt with incompetence and messier scenarios before, but he could usually flip out his ID and haul in everything the Bureau offered to work around and through that. What with being on leave and trespassing on other agents' territory, he knew his performance here was going to be mostly about gut feelings and a great deal of bluffing— bluffing the kidnapper or kidnappers, as well as H and his family to keep them convinced that he could pull this off.

Hoping he was right about the phone bugs and the per-petrator's lack of experience, he drew a deep breath. "Okay, gentlemen, this is what we're going to do...."

Chapter Twelve

"I'm thinking it's going to turn out to be a mistake that you called E.D. and told her that you had car trouble and would be staying the night in town," Jonas told Dylan. "First you plan an impromptu trip to the ranch, but you don't go with them, citing an attorneys' conference you had to deal with before leaving town—"

"It isn't the first time that one of us goes early and the other follows."

"Yeah, but how often do you then have car trouble? It sounds contrived to me."

They were following H in his tiny hybrid back to the Freeman residence, keeping their distance so as not to look as if they were together. H was doing better with his driving; the only reason a cop might stop him now was to order him out of the state for operating a vehicle the size of a shoebox.

"I know it sounded risky to you," Dylan replied. "But it's the one thing that wouldn't make E.D. immediately start worrying. My Navigator is five years old and she's been after me to get a new one. She's normally quite frugal, but she thinks the thing is starting to look embarrassing for a state Supreme Court judge."

Jonas relented and shot him an amused look. "Love is a wonderful thing."

"Yes, it is."

"But if she finds out the truth…death by a thousand paper cuts with her using your marriage license might be welcome."

"That'll never happen."

"You lied to her. Twice. Believe me, I know what deep water you're in."

"What she'll do is lock herself in the bathroom and cry."

"Give me a break," Jonas scoffed.

"She's very protective of me. I'm her knight in shining armor."

If Jonas hadn't caught Dylan's suddenly over-bright eyes, and the way his Adam's apple bobbed up and down as he swallowed hard, he would have bet his friend was trying to pull one over on him. "You're a lucky man," he said with satisfaction for his friend—and more than a little envy.

"Amen to that. So how are you doing with Alyx?"

"Before your call, fine. Terrific. Now? I can't even let myself think about how much damage I've done to our relationship."

"Damn, I'm sorry."

"Me, too. But there wasn't time to dream up anything as creative as you did. I simply told her that I had to go and under no circumstances could she try to contact me."

Dylan grunted. "Smooth, bud, real smooth."

"I was thinking of you, too. I had to shut her down so that she would freeze to where she wouldn't call E.D. You should thank me."

"Forget it. But I might lend Alyx our marriage license to use on you."

Starting to feel more of a bum than he already did, Jonas crossed his arms over his seat belt and chest. "Could we change the subject to something constructive? Tell me how you and H met?"

"Well, aside from being frugal to where he looks like he shops in his grandfather's closet, he's quite the altruist and we both sit on the board of a civic organization that arranges for scholarships for gifted but underprivileged kids. I liked him immediately. Aside from being brilliant, he's unprepossessing, and there's a sweetness in his soul that has always made me worry for him a bit."

"Then why the hell haven't you told him before that he needed more security?"

"Because I was trying not to meddle. Things seemed to be working for them."

"We all live in a twenty-first century version of the Wild West, my friend. Optimism is a luxury. Look at how quickly you moved E.D. and the kids out of harm's way— and you and E.D. are both licensed and skilled with using concealed weapons."

"Believe me, if any harm comes to that boy, I'll never forgive myself."

"None of us will. Just make sure that once this is over he gets help."

"Consider it done."

Jonas accepted and moved on. "After I check Mrs. Freeman's routine regarding service people, I'm going to be asking his housekeeper some pointed questions. You can help by keeping the family out of the kitchen."

Dylan's expression went from distressed to pained. "You think she could be involved?"

"I hope not. They seem as trusting of her as you do of Chris at the ranch."

"If she's anything close to being as reliable and trustworthy as he is, it'll take more than me to keep them from trying to throw you out for putting her under your professional microscope."

"Nothing would please me more than to witness that devotion again."

Maybe Jonas had said she wasn't to call him, but that evening as Alyx was in the middle of packing, she decided that didn't mean she couldn't call E.D. and pick her brain about this sudden turn of events. Reaching for her cell phone, she patted Grace, who was lying with her back to Alyx, determined to ignore the sight of yet another suitcase. E.D., too, had fallen in love, really in love, at a more mature age. With a college-student daughter and high-school-student son, she'd even borne another child with Dylan. If anyone could read between the lines and tell her what on earth Jonas's bizarre behavior this morning had meant, she would know.

She hesitated clicking on E.D.'s name in her address book. It was getting late, but then she remembered the time difference, and was delighted when E.D. picked up immediately. But her pleasure was short-lived.

"You're an answer to a prayer."

Alyx managed a smile. "It's nice to be wanted."

"Good. You can help me stop feeling sorry for myself. We're supposed to have some quiet family time here at the ranch, and Jonas was to follow the kids and me after he finished up some work in town. Then his SUV acted up. The dealer offered him a rental, but he didn't want to drive it all the way down here and back again tomorrow to get his vehicle, so he's spending the night at the house, hoping they'll live up to their promise and he'll be here by midmorning. Just last week I was trying to convince him again to trade it in and get a new model. As much as he drives, I can't bear the thought of him stuck on the road who knows where."

"Well, I'm sorry, but I have confidence that you'll be able to convince him this time."

"You've got that right. So how are you since we last spoke?"

"Oh, I'm afraid I have a worse case of what you've got."

"Dear me. What's Jonas done?"

"E.D., he walked out on me this morning and I don't know what to think about it."

"He *what?*"

"I can't believe it myself, since he'd told me he loved me just an hour before."

"But that's wonderful! I knew it would happen. There's so much fire between you two. It couldn't all be about sex."

"I'm beginning to wish it was, and that we had left well enough alone. I hate feeling like this."

"Tell me all about it," E.D. crooned. "I'm sure it's not as bad as you think. But knowing how competitive you two are, I suspect you're about to tell me that you squabbled."

"Not really. Oh, he asked me how I felt about him moving to Texas, and he was a bit disgruntled because I didn't see how that was easily possible since the promotion he'd hoped for didn't come through. I was trying to figure out what exactly his plan was, only the phone rang and he abruptly left."

"Without even saying goodbye?"

"He kissed me—right after he ordered me not to call him under any circumstances."

"How bizarre is that?"

"Exactly."

"He must have been called back to Washington."

Alyx had considered that, too, but rejected the idea. "Would they do that when he's on leave? I haven't heard anything on the news to suggest a big enough reason."

"Maybe the government has succeeded in keeping it from the press so far. I wonder if Dylan has heard anything?" E.D. mused. "Bet he knows about Jonas's promotion."

"Surely not. Dylan would have told you."

"Not if he gave his word to keep it quiet, at least for a while."

"Oh."

Chuckling, E.D. said, "Now that sounds like you've hit a mental roadblock. There are things that spouses have to keep to themselves from time to time."

"I suppose. Maybe. Okay. I guess I'm simply confused as to why Jonas wouldn't want me to call, unless he was working, in which case he could always turn off the darned phone."

"Unless it's imperative he leaves it on. Just a second." E.D. cooed at her son then came back on. "Judge Junior was ready to be laid down in his crib."

"I'm sorry to be bothering you with this," Alyx sighed.

"Please, you're not. I'm upset for you—and intrigued. Let me ring my darling husband, and I'll see if I can pry anything out of him."

"E.D., you are beyond dear."

"Call you back."

"Why don't they call?"

Sarah Freeman's gaze would haunt Jonas for a long time after this was over. Her eyes weren't just red-rimmed, like her husband's, they were glassy with shock. She was a petite and slender woman who reminded him of a dainty sparrow, easy to overlook on first glance, but who, when observed over time, would prove to possess an appeal for her studiousness and resilience. However, that resilience was fading every minute she was without her firstborn child. Jonas had spent a good while talking to her about her son, her marriage, their life, and he'd been reassured by what he saw and heard. That didn't make telling her the truth any easier.

"There's a good possibility that while there are no listening devices in here, chances are they have been watching and saw something they didn't like," he told her.

"But H got the checks!"

Indeed he had, and with surprising ease. That troubled Jonas somewhat. Harold Freeman could be the living saint Dylan described, but Jonas knew that far too many people were vastly more human, and now he had questions for, if not suspicions about, the teller who'd served him at the bank.

"It's getting dark." Sarah went to the front living-room window and parted the drapes. "Jimbo's condition makes him chilly even in the summer. If they gave us his T-shirt, what's he wearing to stay warm?"

It was all Jonas could do not to yank her away from there. "Mrs. Freeman, why don't you go check on Faith and maybe read her a story? I'm sure she's troubled by having strangers in the house for so long." Particularly two strangers wearing guns, even if they were sensitive enough to hide them by pulling their shirttails over their waistbands.

"Yes, that's a good idea, but…the mall closes in less than two hours."

Jonas couldn't stand it anymore and, crossing to her, he gently but firmly moved her from the window and shut the drapes. "I know what time it is, Mrs. Freeman. Please go to your little girl."

As soon as she did, Jonas gave Dylan a speaking glance and went to the kitchen. He wanted to speak to the Freemans' housekeeper again.

Loretta Saddler just about had the dinner dishes put away. She had insisted on cooking, but everyone had found it a struggle to eat more than a bite. Her figure advertised that she enjoyed feeding her adopted family. Of average height, she had surprisingly bony arms and legs that she didn't try to hide with her short-sleeved white blouse and her denim skirt. Her salt-and-pepper hair was sternly brushed and pinned in a bun at her nape. But there was nothing harsh in the way she watched and fretted over those she cared for. In her early fifties, she'd come to the Freemans only months after burying her husband of thirty years. She said it had been a happy marriage, and Jonas suspected she had transferred the devotion she'd felt for her husband to them.

During his earlier questioning, Jonas had learned she had one son, but geography and complacency had turned them into polite strangers. There was a grandson, who had hung around for a while, but always with a hardship story and his hand out. The last she'd heard, he had joined the army and was deployed overseas.

"Agent Hunter," she said upon spotting him. "I've made a fresh pot of coffee. Would you care for a cup?"

"Jonas," he reminded her for the third time. He eyed the back door's deadbolt lock and the blinds, secured and lowered. "Thank you, that would be great."

"Mr. H and the judge are in the den?"

"Yes, I'll ask them if they need refills. I just wanted to say that I'm sorry we didn't do your dinner more justice."

"A roast makes delicious leftovers. It's understandable that no one has an appetite, but it's my job to make them try to eat."

She removed her amazingly clean white apron and folded it. Then to Jonas's surprise she placed it on top of the basket of other neatly stacked white linens waiting to be washed in the laundry room.

He had to ask. "How can you tell what gets washed and what's clean?"

"Mr. Jonas. Clean things don't sit in a laundry room. They're ironed and put in their place."

He suspected that she was wondering about his upbringing, but at least he'd succeeded in getting her to drop the "Agent" title. With some amusement, he noted that the "Mr. Jonas" made him sound like part of her family.

"You're very fond of Jimbo. This is hitting you as hard as it is his parents and sister." He regretted having to push on wounds, but he had yet to determine if she was manipulating him and was actually part of this kidnapping, or whether she was perhaps being wittingly or unwittingly used herself.

"He's the sweetest boy, gentle and guileless like his father and every bit as smart—you mark my words. Do you know, soon after I started here he saw a news report about conjoined twins being separated, and he sat glued to the television until the program was over. Then as natural as can be he turned to his father and announced that's what he would do when he grew up. The child was all of *four*." Loretta raised her finger to the sky like a prophet. "Faith is a charmer and will steal hearts with her girly-girl ways, but Jimbo is deep water. You'll rarely hear him laugh, and yet his knowing and tender smiles are like a calming hand on your soul."

When Jonas first saw Jimbo's picture, which Sarah Freeman took from a photo album that she stroked like one of her children, he saw a miniature version of his father. He saw a boy who knew he wasn't destined to be sighed over by girls, and was tolerantly looking at the photographer as though saying, "Do what you have to do." The gifted photographer had understood and captured an instant where an old soul had peered from the past through the eyes of a child.

"His condition doesn't frighten him," Jonas said, speaking half to himself.

"No, but he takes it seriously. On his first day of kindergarten he showed his medical bracelet to every member of his class as well as the teacher. He told them that it was important for them to get used to looking for such things when they came upon people needing help."

"I'm looking forward to meeting him."

As soon as she closed the laundry-room door, Loretta grabbed a tissue from a box beside the refrigerator and pressed it to her nose. "God forgive me. When you have a child that only gives you worry, to see a spot of joy like Jimbo taken from those who see the gift he is—well, it shakes your faith."

No wonder that while still a relatively young woman, she had chosen the Freemans as her extended family rather than another husband, or her own flesh and blood.

The ringing phone snapped Jonas out of his ruminations. "Sorry," he muttered and rushed to the den.

H sat frozen, staring at the phone. Jonas pointed to the speaker button and held a cautionary hand up in case Sarah or Loretta ran in forgetting that it was imperative they remain quiet.

H did as directed and forced out a croaklike, "Hello?"

"Man, you were told, don't call the police."

"I didn't!"

"Yeah, so what was that black Navigator turning into your street after you today?"

"What?" Wide-eyed with panic, H's gaze locked with Jonas's.

Jonas sliced his fingers across his throat shaking his head vehemently, then mouthed, *you don't know.*

"M-mister…this street has some fifteen or eighteen houses on it. What are you talking about?"

After a pause, the caller snapped, "You're lying."

"I'm not! Please, let me talk to my son. I have the money."

"I need to think about this."

"But the mall is closing!"

The caller disconnected.

H dropped the receiver as though it was a snake. From the kitchen doorway, Loretta muffled a sob behind a handful of tissues. Beside him, Sarah stood frozen, with tears pouring down her bloodless face. While he was aware of them all, and Dylan's worried stare, Jonas replayed what had just occurred in his mind. Slowly he began nodding.

"He's going to call back." It didn't surprise him that everyone gaped at him as though he was an evangelist suddenly speaking in tongues.

"Why would he?" Dylan asked, as though urging him to take back what he felt was an inappropriate promise. "You heard him. He saw us."

"Think. Hear what he said. H, your response was perfect. Yeah, he saw us follow H into the street. He didn't see us turn into this driveway. Wherever he was staked out, his view was limited. What does that tell you?" No one wanted to offer a guess. "He would attract attention. He doesn't belong on a street like this unless he's mowing lawns or repairing something. He's also not a pro. I'll go so far as to surmise that if this isn't his first attempt at kidnapping, it's close to it. He didn't have the guts to see if he'd got blocked in and taken." Jonas looked at Jimbo's father. "Take a deep breath. Right now he's pacing and second-guessing himself. In a few minutes, he *will* call back."

But the ringing began that instant—only it wasn't the Freeman phone. As the others started, Dylan swore under his breath and fumbled with his cell in his pocket.

"Shut that thing off!" Jonas growled.

"Sorry. I must have hit a button somehow." Dylan looked at the screen and he closed his eyes. "Jonas, it's E.D."

"Ignore it. If he calls back while you're talking to her we're cooked."

"I can go out to the garage."

"And say what to her? She's probably already called your house and knows you're not there."

His head bowed, Dylan nodded. Looking as though he would rather cut off a finger, he did as directed.

Silence fell and lingered, an uncomfortable presence in the room. Then the phone began ringing again.

H glanced at Jonas and then depressed the speaker button again. "Hello?"

"Tonight has been cancelled," the caller said.

"You can't!" H cried. "I told you, I have the money. Give me my—"

"Shut up! This is your last chance," the caller said with more control. "It'll be tomorrow, everything else is the same, but the time. It's now at three o'clock. Got it? You try anything, what follows is your fault."

Alyx sat on the barstool at the counter where she'd sat with Jonas only hours ago and stared at her phone, willing it to ring. No disrespect to E.D. or lack of gratitude, but she willed Jonas to call first. She would be so disappointed, even embarrassed, if it turned out that Dylan knew what was going on and shared it with E.D., while she sat here clueless. Maybe Dylan's history with Jonas went back farther, but in her opinion, once you tell someone you love them—

At the sound of the ringing phone, she reached out too fast and hard, struck it with the back of her hand, and unintentionally sent it careening off the counter. "No!" she cried, racing after it. What if it hit the floor so hard it broke?

Scooping it off the tile floor, she answered on the third ring. "Yes?" she gasped.

"You sound as anxious as I feel," E.D. told her.

Alyx brushed her hair back from her face and wondered what that meant. "You didn't find out *anything?*"

"Worse. He's not answering the house phone, nor his cell."

"Maybe he's on his way there to surprise you."

E.D. made a negative sound. "Between Dani's Internet photo surprises and Trey's secret affair, Dylan and I decided surprises were off the table for the foreseeable future. No, something isn't right."

Alyx couldn't accept that. If possible, that was worse than being the only person in the dark. "It's my fault. I've just put ideas in your head."

"You didn't have to," her Deputy DA friend told her. "We don't abuse the phones. We're too mindful of each other's workload. If one calls the other and can't get through, we call back within five minutes or text message. It's been almost thirty minutes since I rang his cell, and he is not home."

Or couldn't answer? As soon as she thought that, Alyx rejected the thought.

"I'm about to call Chris and ask him to—wait! He's calling me now. Back with you shortly."

"Did you hear that?" Alyx said to the dead phone in her hand. "Dylan is calling her. Why aren't you calling *me?*"

For the next two minutes, Alyx sat, wondering what was coming next. It was going to be difficult news, she just felt it.

The phone rang.

Without waiting for Alyx's greeting, E.D. said numbly, "Jonas is with Dylan."

Chapter Thirteen

Parke's flight was almost thirty minutes late, leaving Alyx with less than an hour to hug her cousin, return her keys to her and catch her own flight back to Texas. That wasn't a bad thing; she was in no mood to go into prolonged explanations. Like E.D., she was worried sick about what was going on back home; unlike E.D., she was also furious and disappointed.

Behind the glass wall partition, Alyx watched Parke sweep through customs, a svelte, long-legged and exotic specimen in her leopard tunic, black leggings and matching leopard-and-patent leather heels. Alyx had dressed for comfort and safety, which made her feel colorless in her white cotton tunic over loose white cotton slacks. And while Parke's raven mane flowed to her shoulder blades in a wild sea of waves, Alyx had secured her hair in a single braid down her back.

"Alyx, my darling," Parke crooned as she emerged from the rotating doors, oblivious to the heads she turned. Arms wide, she embraced Alyx and kissed the air near both of her cheeks in the European fashion. "*Ciao, bella.* Don't you look all fresh and untouched? Rather like Audrey Hepburn about to take her vows of celibacy. What was the name of that movie?"

"Parke, please don't tease—or embarrass me in front of the entire airport."

"Embarrass? I'm flattering you, silly. It's quite an appealing look what with your wounded eyes and all. Can you wear those blinding diamond studs at a nunnery? I might look into that since I've turned down what is probably the last decent pass I'll ever get in this lifetime."

Parke's flourish for exaggeration was as ingrained in her style as was her dramatic art. Alyx grumbled, "Why don't you just mew 'Help,' and see how many men trample each other to offer you their services? Or wait for the drive home, since you know perfectly well no less than three state troopers will stop you on your way up to Sedona, though none of them for speeding."

"If it's only three, I'm going to look into plastic surgery, but thank you for the ego stroke." Parke ducked her head to peer under Alyx's lashes. "What's the latest from points east?"

They'd last talked after Parke had landed at JFK in New York, and Alyx was taking Grace out one more time before leaving for Phoenix. "He's in Texas!" Alyx had declared then. "E.D. finally got Dylan to return her calls. There's some kind of situation going on that he wouldn't expand on, but you can bet it's dangerous."

"What—is Mystery Man actually into mysterious work? Is he a cop or something?"

"FBI," Alyx admitted. "We met the last time Dylan asked him for help. Remember E.D.'s case?"

"I do, indeed," Parke had replied with new admiration. "It sounds as though he's capable, and if it is his job—"

"Not right now it isn't," Alyx interjected. "He's on leave, you know, like off duty. If headquarters gets wind of this—whatever this is—he won't have to decide whether to retire or not, they'll fire him!"

Now Alyx told Parke, "E.D. wants me to come out to the ranch and wait with her. I think I'd rather go home."

"And do what, pout because Special Agent Jonas didn't tell you himself? Worry yourself sick because he's sticking out his professional and physical neck, or worse, for a friend?"

Shooting her a quelling glance, Alyx replied, "It's Special Agent Hunter, and is this your idea of familial support?"

Parke looped her arm through Alyx's. "Which way to your gate?"

Alyx gestured right with her free hand.

"Let's walk." As they started, her cousin continued. "I think E.D. has the right idea. Jonas thinks you're still here. When he sees you came home out of concern for him, he'll sweep you into his arms and all will be forgiven."

Alyx was glad for the company, but Parke couldn't be more incorrect in her conclusions. "Jonas knows I was booking a flight back for today and we didn't part on the most reassuring terms."

"You fought?"

"We hadn't gotten to that point, but when the call came, we'd just…stumbled."

"And he left without even a goodbye?"

Alyx tried, but couldn't deny the gesture he'd made. "He kissed me."

"The rat."

"It was not a gentle or polite kiss."

"If he comes back in one piece, murder him."

Unable to help herself, Alyx laughed. "So I'm an idiot, but this is crazy. I didn't ask for any of this. I was having an affair with a sexy man. Life was perfect."

"Then you fell in love."

Realizing they'd already reached her gate, Alyx stopped. "This is me."

"In more ways than one." Parke's smile was all warmth and concern. "Listen to me, favorite relative. As terrified as you are, think about E.D. She's got their baby and her other two children who might be in danger of losing what sounds to me a seriously hot—for a judge—father and stepdad. Go for her sake. If nothing else works for you, at least you have that."

"You're right."

"Did I do you any good luring you up to Sedona?"

Smiling, Alyx lifted her injured arm nearly straight in the air. "I didn't have time to buy Shar a gift in gratitude. I don't suppose you could see your way to give me your favorite-cousin discount so I can present her one of your smaller paintings?"

"She is going to be ecstatic, and I know exactly which would suit her." Coaxing Alyx to turn, she pointed into a small gallery featuring Arizona artisans. "See the watercolor of the yellow cactus blooms and the two sweet baby bunnies?"

"Is that yours, too? Parke, I'm so proud of you. You're for sale at airports. You have arrived!"

"Be careful about how loudly you say that," Parke drawled. "But what I meant was that I have one at the house with pink blossoms and a mother fox nursing her two pups that I know Shar would love."

"Great. It's a deal." As they began announcing the early seating of her flight, Alyx hugged her cousin. "Go. Call me and let me know what I owe you. Grace knows you're coming and probably has so many nose prints on the windows that you'll be cleaning for a week."

Parke smiled, only to grow somber. "Try not to worry."

"Too late."

"Well, then try to understand him, even as you're trying not to love him. It sounds like you fell for an honorable and principled man." Parke kissed her cousin's cheek and immediately wiped away the touch of lipstick she left behind. "Oh, I brought you a little something. Had I only known this bent toward dressing like a postulant it should have been rosary beads."

"Hilarious." But Alyx lifted an eyebrow as she accepted and opened the leather pouch, then drew out a jeweler's box. Removing the lid, she gasped at the delicate eighteen-carat-gold Byzantine-design bangle.

"I've always thought you have the hands and wrists for ornamentation. It's an impossible dream for someone in my trade."

"But look at what those hands create. Parke, thank you so much. I'll cherish it."

"Call me when you get news. I don't care the hour."

* * *

It was closing in on three in the afternoon when Alyx pulled into the Justiss Ranch and keyed the code that E.D. had given her over the phone. The flight had been on time and traffic relatively light; nevertheless, Alyx felt as though she'd been the one to fly half around the earth, not Parke. Having had little sleep was also part of the problem.

Seeing E.D. hurry from the house, Alyx's heart lifted, until she saw that there were no other vehicles visible except E.D.'s silver Navigator. Then, as she emerged from her white BMW and saw the signs of concern and stress on her friend's face, Alyx's heart sank anew.

"No further contact?"

"A little, but you won't like it any more than I did." E.D. hugged her and led her toward the house. "He called just after you and I last talked and said maybe it would be over later this afternoon."

Whatever "it" was. "No explanation? Not even a hint of what or where they are?"

Holding the storm door open for her, E.D. shook her head mournfully. "Nothing. Alyx, since I didn't know how bad things could get, I haven't said anything to the kids. I know I'm asking a great deal from you, but when they're around would you—"

Alyx raised her hand. "Say no more. I understand completely." But once inside, Alyx saw no sign of the children or heard anything. "Where is everyone?"

"Chris is being a sweetheart and has taken Dani and Mac for a trail ride. 'Two,' as Judge Junior calls himself, is having a much welcome nap. Much welcome for Mommy."

"I'm assuming you cautioned Chris, as well?"

"Of course. In fact, he knows everything we do. Dylan would want that."

Everything—such as it was. Alyx suppressed her agitation by taking in her surroundings and noting the changes since she'd last been here. The "cottage" had been in Dylan's family for generations, and additions had been made to its original two or three rooms to accommodate the growing Justiss family when they weren't at their home in Austin. Alyx's favorite spot was the state-of-the-art kitchen that looked out onto a gorgeous patio complete with a huge smoker-barbecue pit, a chiminea for keeping cozy during chilly evenings or for roasting marshmallows, and comfortable cedar furniture that foreman Chris Coats was building as time allowed.

"Can I get you a cup of coffee or tea?" E.D. asked.

Alyx shook her head and put her purse down on the kitchen counter. Although she looked too young and trim in her worn denim slacks and pink blouse to be a mother three times over, E.D. appeared ready to collapse.

"I've been sitting for hours. You're the one who should be waited on. Why don't you have a seat and I'll get you…what's your pleasure?"

"My husband."

She spoke so softly, Alyx could have imagined the words, but she knew her friend had probably spoken them involuntarily. There were couples who were simply meant for each other, and E.D. and Dylan were one of those. Crossing over to her, Alyx hugged her again.

"I'm going to get you a glass of wine. I've decided I

need one, too. It doesn't sound like I need to worry about driving anytime soon."

"There's a chardonnay open in the main refrigerator. But if you don't care for the vineyard, there are other choices in the wine cooler."

"Considering your impeccable taste in every other department, I think what's here will be great," she said opening the double-door refrigerator.

As she chose two glasses from the cabinet E.D. directed her to, E.D. said, "Forgive me for not asking sooner—how's Parke?"

"Sassy as ever. But her heart is still gold." Alyx extended her hand across the kitchen bar's granite counter. "She brought me this."

E.D. formed her mouth into a silent O. "It's exquisite…and looks old."

"She was too generous."

"She loves you, which is a good thing since you don't have much family besides each other. You also made it possible for her to have peace of mind while she was gone."

Alyx handed her friend one of the half-filled glasses, then gently touched hers to E.D.'s. "Here's to a happy ending to our waiting."

"And how."

"E.D., I hope Jonas didn't get Dylan into anything."

"Hon, Jonas came *here,* not the other way around. It's obvious Dylan needed him."

"That's probably a technicality." Hearing the cynicism in her voice, Alyx sipped her wine and focused on the coolness and creamy flavor, hoping it would ease the bitterness that kept rising inside her. "I'm thinking how much more you have at risk than I do."

"You can't do that to yourself—weighing, judging one relationship against someone else's. Shortchanging what you and Jonas have doesn't make my love with Dylan any more or less than it is."

Alyx closed her eyes. "I just wish he could have been more honest with me. Shared something after Dylan's call to make the declaration he'd made earlier feel as though he meant it."

E.D. reached over and touched the back of her hand. "He's new at this, Alyx. I dare say as new at it as you are. What he had with Claudia was a brief aberration. Dylan told me. Jonas got caught up with ambition and social standing…he intended to move up in the Bureau and you know what government life is like—image and appearances. But that was all too small for Claudia, and—hasn't he told you any of this?"

"Our communicating hasn't quite been, um, as verbal as you might think."

E.D. laughed with wicked delight. "I'm all for more sensory communicating. But seriously, Alyx, I'm guessing that Jonas hasn't told you more about his ex because he doesn't think the matter worth much time or energy. They didn't fit."

"We fit. You know we do."

Alyx wrapped her arms around her waist. "Yes, but he has a son with the woman."

"A son whom he loves and is proud of and sees when he can. But kids grow up and find their own lives, and Blake is in that growing independent age when a parent, ready or not, has to stand back and give the nestling room to spread his wings. He'll always be there for Blake if needed, just as he dropped everything for his professional responsibility. But it's you he aches for. Trust me, I have sensed this for some time."

If only. "You're a born nurturer," Alyx told her with open admiration.

"It comes easily enough when you're happy."

Alyx fingered her bracelet and thought of the last several days she and Jonas had shared. They'd begun building a routine. "I felt a glimmer of that happiness, and then it went cold on me."

"Did it? Are you sure?" E.D. touched her glass to Alyx's once again. "Life intrudes sometimes. But when it backs off and things calm down—" she looked out back, but what she was seeing was clearly farther away than the boundaries of the ranch "—what remains is all a heart can hold. Wait and see."

"Wait," Jonas murmured. "Wait and see what she does. She could simply be a lazy kid willing to spend a dollar on gas to gain a closer parking space. No, she's our girl. She's not interested in any aisles except the one where H is parked and the one she goes down so she can circle back."

He and Dylan were parked two aisles behind H. They'd arrived minutes after him and with many mothers and wives heading home to prepare dinner, it was relatively easy to find a spot with a good view.

They'd developed their plan for delivering the money last night and reviewed it several times this morning, looking for flaws and solutions in case of exigent circumstances. Jonas had even asked the Freemans one more time whether they wouldn't consider calling in the police or FBI, but neither would hear of it for fear that it decreased their son's safety.

"You've been right about these people so far," Sarah told him. "And Dylan is here, willing to risk his own safety, not to mention his career, because of you. That speaks volumes as far as we're concerned."

"Any last doubts, comments or suggestions?" Jonas said to Dylan as H left his small hybrid. He all but groaned as H locked it, then remembered his directive to leave it unlocked in case Jimbo got free and tried to get inside, and unlocked it.

"Yeah, I think my deodorant almost quit on me," Dylan replied.

"Think about how H feels. The poor guy hasn't been in a mall since how old as a kid? We'll be lucky if he doesn't collapse in a dead faint the moment he sees that Victoria's Secret display window diagonally across from the fast-food spot. He was shaking so badly as he climbed into his car back at the house, I swear I saw the thing rocking." He watched H cross the drop off and fire lane and step up to the mall's sidewalk. "Heckuva nice guy."

"He said some nice things about you."

All of which would change, Jonas thought, if they botched this. Then the older white pickup truck sped up and came down to stop behind H's compact car.

"Mission Control, we have contact," Dylan drawled. "But I don't see Jimbo."

"He's been told to lie down on the passenger seat and keep out of sight. See how the driver keeps looking over and down? She's not singing, and I have a hunch she's not talking to herself. Now check her hands. She's done all of the driving with her left hand, even the turns. She's got her other hand on the boy to make him stay put."

Jonas ordered, "Duck!" as the shaggy-haired brunette twisted around to check out the parking lot.

"Okay, my hunch is as soon as H emerges from the mall, she's going to order Jimbo out and she's going to go pick up her partner."

"At the same entrance?" Dylan asked. "H will be able to get the license number."

Rising again, Jonas said, "Look at her, she's a teenager. That tells you the person inside is likely to be, too. What I am worried about is that she might try to run H over before she picks up her pal at the north or south side of the parking lot. Or if it goes too smoothly, keeps the boy." A chill swept through Jonas. "Change of plans. E.D. wants you to get a new SUV anyway."

Dylan did a double take. "Say you don't mean—you want me to hit her? With Jimbo in there?"

"Key the ignition, move it," Jonas said, getting out. "Hurry. I've got to get inside. Hit her in her right rear wheel, you bend it, or at least cause the tire to go flat. Act apologetic until you get her out of the truck. Take my badge and tuck it onto your wallet. Flash it then and force her against the truck. Have you got any duct tape in this thing?"

"Yeah," Dylan said, opening the middle armrest compartment.

"Tape her hands and lean her over H's car, then start calling 911 like there's no tomorrow. Try to remember to tell them an FBI agent is inside taking down the other perp. Go!"

"What if she has a gun?" Dylan muttered as Jonas walked away.

It was always a possibility, but Jonas thought if anyone had one, it was the person collecting the money.

"Go!"

Jonas slipped on the borrowed baseball cap to keep the sunlight from brightening his hair and catching her attention fast. Although he moved with some speed, his gait was gangly, and he pretended to be more interested in finding a quarter on the ground than scoping out the place like a SWAT team member.

Just as he opened the first door of the mall entryway, Dylan struck the pickup. The girl screamed and started cursing, and he glanced back only long enough to see that not only did Dylan quickly have things under control, Jimbo was scrambling out the passenger door.

Quickly making his way through the second door, he saw things were not going as well inside. H was still at the chicken restaurant's order counter trying to buy an empty cup and lid. The girl waiting on him was giving him a hard time and enjoying it.

"Okay, okay," H snapped, pulling out his wallet. "Give me an ice water." He flung a dollar across the counter and, when she returned, all but snatched the cup out of her hand. His face was beet-red as he ripped off the lid and dumped the contents into a planter.

The girl watched, snickering.

Jonas narrowed his eyes. As concerned as he was that H was beginning to panic, the girl with the dirty-blond ponytail troubled him. Not only was she being rude, she didn't care who saw that. Customer service was going down in many fields, but this brought the problem to a new low.

H stuffed the plastic bag into the cup in clear view of anyone watching—exactly what Jonas had cautioned him about—then forced it into the trash container. As he strode back to the mall doors, the girl at the fast-food counter called to him.

"Hey, mister, you forgot your change! Hey! Big spender, you forgot your change!"

Unbelievable, thought Jonas. Then it hit him—this was a diversion.

Sure enough, everyone was watching the girl's outrageous behavior. She tore off her apron and visor-style hat, flung them somewhere behind her, and ran after H out the door. No one was paying attention to the skinny guy in the custodian's outfit who arrived with his cart and lifted off the trash-can lid. But Jonas did, and once the guy snatched the black plastic bag out of the gray bin and headed for the exit, too, Jonas gave chase.

There were three of them, not just two.

He was so close behind him that the outer door hadn't yet closed. Jonas pushed it wide, saw that both the guy and ex-counter girl had frozen in their tracks, seeing the commotion at the white pickup. Coming up behind the guy, he yelled.

"Hey! You dropped your wallet!"

Startled, the guy turned and Jonas punched him hard in the stomach, causing him to bend in half and fall to his knees, the bag dropping out of his grasp. The girl's reactions were better. She grabbed the bag, and pivoted to run, but Jonas grabbed her wrist and twisted it so hard behind her back, she, too, dropped the sack and screamed.

"FBI—down to the ground. Down! Both of you."

People were beginning to collect and a security guard emerged with his gun drawn. "Everybody freeze!"

"Special Agent Jonas Hunter, FBI," he told the guard as he complied with the order. "These two and the girl by the white pickup are kidnappers of that blond-haired boy being held by his father. Call for backup."

The wide-eyed guard nodded, but said, "You stay put, too."

"No problem. But I need to inform you that there's an automatic tucked in at the small of my back. Don't get nervous and shoot the wrong people."

Across the way, H was hugging his son and Dylan had finished duct-taping the girl's hands behind her back and was urging her to join the other two Jonas had dropped. He brought the tape toward them with his hands up. "Judge Dylan Justiss, officer."

The security guard gaped and lowered both his gun and radio. "I seen your picture in the paper. It is you. What the heck...?"

"It's a long story, but we're sure glad you arrived when you did. We expected two, not three, suspects. I have a feeling a reward and citation are about to make you a happy man."

Chapter Fourteen

"You busted my Navigator," Dylan said as they climbed into Jonas's rental car. "The least you could do is drive me to the ranch."

Jonas waved the ignition key, rejecting the accusation. "I told you to do it. You were behind the wheel. Free will."

It was dusk by the time the felons were questioned, the story unraveled, the identities of the suspects discovered, arrests made, and Jonas, Dylan and Harold Freeman had supplied their full statements. Early on at headquarters, the chief of police offered an escort for Jimbo to be taken home or to the hospital for a checkup, but he wouldn't let go of his father and so H recounted his story with his son on his lap. Father and son were then given a ride home. The chief handpicked the detectives to handle the assignment and assured H that he wouldn't be inconvenienced with a trip downtown again. Any and all interviews prior to the court hearings could be handled at his home or at Digit Dynamics' offices.

Although H thanked Jonas and Dylan profusely and took full blame for any rules and regulations broken, the chief was less deferential to Dylan and even less so to Jonas. The terms *freelance vigilante* and *mercenary* were spoken. But in the end, no blood was spilled, except by Jonas, the victim was safe, and H had his money back. The chief ultimately said he had all he needed for the time being and provided them with a squad-car ride to an airport car-rental service. That was because in the collision, part of the pickup had pierced the SUV's radiator and it wasn't going anywhere but to the dealership service center via tow truck.

"Besides, I want to get to Alyx's house," Jonas added. "She should be there by now if she got that flight, and I want to tell her about what happened before she sees it on the news."

"What about me?" Dylan countered. "E.D. is probably already in the bathroom sobbing her poor eyes out."

Muttering under his breath, Jonas relented, shoved the key in the ignition and hissed in pain. "You drive," he told Dylan, holding his bandaged hand.

Dylan drove them to the ranch—most of the way wearing a self-satisfied smile on his face. By the time they approached the secured gate, Jonas had told him that he was heartily sick of that grin.

At the gate, Dylan pressed the intercom button and then keyed the code for the gates to open. "It's us," he told Chris.

"Welcome home."

"Everything okay in there?"

"They all held up pretty well. Saw y'all on TV."

"Probably won't be the last time," Jonas said, thinking of the reprimands or worse that he had to look forward to. "Remind me to borrow a work glove from you for the drive back so I'm not blind with pain by the time I get to Alyx's."

"Sure thing," Dylan said with an agreeable nod.

Dylan's family was pouring out onto the porch as they pulled up, but what got Jonas's attention was the familiar BMW parked behind E.D.'s SUV.

"That's Alyx's car."

"Well, what do you know," Dylan said.

E.D. and the kids attacked Dylan, leaving an open path through which he could see one more person standing on the porch. With all of the lanterns and security lights on, Alyx looked ethereal in white, standing very still, her expression even more serious.

"You got a flight back," he said, stepping closer.

She nodded.

"So Parke made it home okay?"

She nodded again.

Not knowing how to begin properly, or end the aching in his chest and throat, Jonas swallowed and blurted out, "I'm sorry, love. I wish I could have told you, but—" he spread his arms in helplessness "—this is the business sometimes."

"I hate your business."

"At the moment I'm not too wild about it myself. But it turned out okay, which you probably already heard on TV."

"Oh, yes. There was little else mentioned on the evening news."

He'd never wanted her more than when she started arching that dark-winged eyebrow and going disdainful.

He stepped up onto the porch and that's when she saw his bandaged hand.

"You're hurt!"

"It's nothing much." Jonas shrugged. "The second girl, the little tiger with the ponytail, crunched me with her combat boot when I bent to pick up the cap I'd borrowed that came off during the scuffling." He glanced at her from under his eyebrows, hoping he looked pitiful and that she'd melt a little for him. "It could use a kiss to make it better. In fact, so could I."

Instead, Alyx kept studying him. Finally, she said, "Once I heard that you were all safe, I was thinking about just getting in my car and leaving, but I decided I wanted to hear you say it again. Just once more, even if you only half mean it."

Hadn't she heard him a second ago? He'd called her "love." While that was probably considered a mere endearment, and not a declaration, he'd thought it was an excellent start. He would have preferred for them to be alone before he got to the really good stuff.

"I'll say it a hundred times if you'll take me with you."

Exhaling, she stepped into his arms and hugged him fiercely.

"Easy, babe. Don't hurt your shoulder."

"You scared me."

He knew it. He could feel it coming from her in waves. He'd made her relive her own terror and potential death. But now it was time to celebrate life, and if she didn't know how to start, he would have to show her. Lifting her chin with his good hand, he locked his mouth to hers.

Did she shudder with relief or pleasure or did he? Maybe

it was both of them. All the better, he thought, bringing her lower body closer so she could know that he'd missed her during their time apart with all of his being.

"I love you, Alyx. Take me home so we can talk, and do this, and…just be."

Reaching up to touch her lips to his more gently, she said, "Let's go."

E.D., not Dylan, tried to encourage them to stay, Alyx noted with amusement and complete understanding. She hugged E.D. and thanked her for keeping her sane, and then kissed Dylan's cheek.

"I'm grateful you were there with him."

"I hope he was worth saving," Dylan replied with an evil grin.

"In that case," Jonas told him, "you can worry about returning the rental yourself."

"Two ride in Dada's caw," Judge Junior shouted in glee from his perch in Dylan's arms.

Jonas laughed all the way to the passenger door of the BMW.

"You two shouldn't be allowed to spend more than ten minutes together at a time," Alyx said after taking the driver's seat. As they exited the ranch and turned onto the farm-to-market road, she concluded, "You bring out the juvenile delinquent in each other."

"I was paying him back for keeping it a secret that you were down here. Do you know how sick I was, thinking it would be another two hours before I got to your house? But I had already asked to borrow a glove because I was determined to do it." Jonas sat facing her as much as the seat belt would allow and stroked her hair. "I like it this way."

Alyx sighed. "Tell me what the news story didn't, Jonas. I need to purge this tension inside me. How did you two get involved with this Freeman family, and, please God, tell me that poor little boy is really all right?"

"Physically, he came through it as well as we could have hoped. You probably saw the brief shot of him on TV in the dirty men's-size T-shirt. It was clear he needed a bath the instant he came home, maybe two, considering the number of insect bites on him. As for mentally, he's a tough little dude, and I don't mean macho, mean stuff. I mean he's a little old man in a kid's body. If there's anything needing tending, he's fortunate that his father is on par with some of the richest people on the planet. Not too educated yet when it comes to understanding how low and mean people can get when they want what you have without working or paying for it, but that's a worry for another day."

"And so Dylan knew him? E.D. didn't really remember."

"Yeah, they've sat on some of the same boards, and Dylan advised him on occasional legal questions. H—he has hated his name for as long as he could remember— admitted that when they first realized Jimbo was grabbed that Dylan was the only person he felt would not treat him like a commodity—or meal ticket."

"How sad," Alyx said. "Everyone wants to be filthy rich, but no one realizes what that does to your life." She glanced at Jonas. "And so naturally Dylan thought of his favorite G-man."

"Could you have said no?"

"Absolutely not. That doesn't mean the floor didn't drop

out from under me when I realized you were the chosen one. And it was worse when Mr. Freeman admitted he compromised everyone's safety because he needed to know and implicitly trust the people he was dealing with." Alyx gripped the steering wheel so tightly her hands ached. "What if the kidnappers were pros? What if there had been a whole organization for hire?"

"I know," Jonas said quietly.

He didn't need this right now. Alyx knew that and quickly apologized. "But do tell me how these young people found this family. I didn't know he existed. I'd heard of the company, but figured it was based in Dallas or San Antonio."

"Ah. This part is fascinating for someone who likes analysis and psychology as much as you do. It turns out the girl in the pickup truck was going with the guy who did the calling and planning, but before they were a couple, she dated the housekeeper's grandson."

Alyx groaned. "It's always someone you know, even indirectly. Not six degrees of separation, but the same concept."

"Yeah. Loretta, the housekeeper, was shattered when she heard. She hasn't seen her grandson in a couple of years. He decided to pull his life together and joined the military and is deployed in Iraq. But during Loretta's first year with the family, he would come begging for money, so obviously he talked enviously of the Freemans."

"And where does the other girl, the one with obvious sociopath issues, come in?"

"She was the first girl's current roommate. Actually, they all share the same apartment."

"Did you learn what they planned to do with the money?"

"They already had reservations paid for with a stolen

credit card for three seats to the Caribbean. They intended to live the good life."

"Which would be short, considering how fast the money would flow through their fingers."

Jonas yawned. "I've been craving a drink for hours, but I swear if I had one in-hand right now, in two sips I'd be unconscious." He reached over to stroke her thigh. "I bet if you pulled over, you'd know how to wake me up?"

Laughing softly, Alyx shook her head. "Forget it. I'll bet the chief put out notice that if any of his people so much as see you accidentally drop a penny and not retrieve it, they're to arrest you for littering. I'm not touching you until I have you safely behind a locked door."

"Yeah?" Jonas's grin was brighter than the moonlight. "What do you have planned for me then?"

"Probably fill a tub for you and let you soak for an hour, then scrub you down in the shower, considering some of the company you've been keeping."

Lifting his arm to smell his shirtsleeve, he grunted. "I'll pay to have your car detailed tomorrow, too."

When they arrived at her place, Alyx insisted they leave their luggage in the trunk. There wasn't anything in their bags that she couldn't provide inside, or that they couldn't do without.

Jonas's heavy-lidded eyes had her running him that bath as promised and he unceremoniously stripped beside her and eased in, groaning, until he was chest-deep in the lightly scented sea-salt water. When she turned on the hot-tub jets, he dropped his head back and closed his eyes.

"Don't wake me until I'm the consistency of the last raisin in a box of cereal," he told her.

Alyx kissed him tenderly. "Enjoy. I'm going to turn down the bed and make you that drink—or do you think a pain pill is more necessary?"

"What's necessary is for us to talk. Not about the FBI, or the kidnapping—"

"Or when you have to return to Sedona," Alyx added, already dreading that time without him even if it was only for a few more weeks.

He looked at her as though she'd lost her mind. "I'm not going back. Are you trying to get rid of me? H said he took me from someone else with a need and that he's responsible to see that Zane doesn't suffer financially for that. It's just a matter of me doing the paperwork and telling him a figure."

Alyx's heart literally did a jitterbug between her breasts.

It was then that Jonas spotted her bracelet and with a soapy hand he took hold of her wrist. "Whoa. Who is this from?"

"Another very generous person."

"Male or female?"

"It's from Parke," she said to put him out of his misery. "Jonas..." She leaned closer and picked up a natural sponge, wet it, and stroked it over his chest in soothing circles. "If you're still interested, I'd like to try talking again about you moving to Texas."

He caressed her cheek with his thumb. "I can't do it."

Blinking, she receded a bit. "Oh. Because of the employment situation, right?"

"No. I could find something. I'm not worried about that."

"Then why? Jonas, I love you," she whispered, resting her forearms on the tub's edge. "I've never said that to another man, if you can believe that."

"Then why won't you marry me?"

Confused, she shook her head. "I never said I wouldn't, but you have to ask me first."

"Excuse me," he replied. "I distinctly remember you saying—and I quote—'You're the last man I'd marry.'"

Alyx bowed her head in shame. "I do wish your memory would fail you this once. That declaration wasn't about you, it was about me and my flaws."

Grimacing as though in pain, he asked, "Can you get me a Band-Aid? Please?"

She didn't see any blood, but Alyx quickly went to the vanity and returned with one. "Here, let me get the paper off so you don't accidentally get that bandage wet. There…now where do you want it?"

Jonas took it from her and held it over her left ring finger. "Until I can replace this with something slightly more respectable, Alyx, my real love, my only love, my last love…will you marry me?"

Tears flooded her eyes and spilled down her cheeks. "Yes, my darling, beloved G-man. I will."

After watching him awkwardly secure the Band-Aid, she kissed him and kissed him again. The tears continued, wetting his cheeks and mixing with the equally hot and salty bathwater.

When they finally parted to catch their breaths, Jonas teased, "What is it about bathrooms with you and E.D.?"

"It's about realizing what's precious to us and what we can't bear the thought of losing."

Jonas stroked his thumb over her kiss-swollen lips. "You won't ever lose me, Alyx. I promise."

Epilogue

The wedding took place in the spring, and while that seemed to Jonas an eternity before he could make the woman of his dreams his, there were times that he thought it a miracle that it had happened at all. And all of the blame fell on his shoulders. Alyx would have been happy to elope; she actually suggested it periodically between his August proposal and the April day when she locked him out of her hotel room because she was getting into her gown.

Standing in his own room in the suite provided by Mr. and Mrs. H. Freeman, Jonas felt awe, humility and inconceivable pride that Alyx had borne the whirlwind changes in their lives so graciously.

It had begun with the stunning request by H that he become the head of security for his family. This came the day after Jonas had drafted him an outline of what he really should do to protect his loved ones, himself and his business. After the shock had passed, the real planning started. Jonas was to oversee the building of a compound which would include a new home for the Freemans and a house for him and Alyx, as well as quarters for other security personnel, a larger garage with apartments above for the chauffeurs, a communications center, dog kennel— the list was daunting. It was a request a corporation would be challenged to undertake, and Jonas had politely declined even before speaking with Alyx about it. He wouldn't consider putting her through all that, asking her to give up a home she loved, living in a house that would never really be hers, and also having to live as a target and under the same rules as everyone else.

With deep gratitude he thanked H and recommended a few companies he knew that were well versed in this kind of endeavor. H had listened patiently and said, "But I don't know those people, Jonas, and I don't want to know them. This is personal and I want to retain as much of the life we had before as possible. I know you understand that. Would you allow me to speak with Alyx?"

Knowing he had no right to make a decision for her, Jonas brought Alyx to H's home and everything was laid out for her. Her first response was to quip to Jonas.

"So this is what you do all day when I'm in court."

But, oh, his darling was proud. She struggled with keeping her composure, and H discreetly left the room looking distraught that he had upset her with his request. Only, as soon as they were alone, Alyx had gone into Jonas's arms and kissed him.

"You are an amazing man, Jonas. I don't know the half

of what I'm seeing, and I worry for your workload, but this is a chance of a lifetime, as well as the supreme compliment in your profession to be offered this. You have to take it."

"The greatest compliment," he'd replied, humbled, "is watching you open your heart to me."

And now, midway through all the construction and interviewing for personnel, and arranging for equipment— their wedding day had arrived. He couldn't wait to see his bride. H had offered a Vera Wang gown. "Sarah says she's tops," he'd confided to Alyx. Jonas's always-with-a-comeback darling had been left speechless.

A knock at the door brought Jonas out of his daydreaming and he called, "Come in!"

"I've got a getaway car posted outside the kitchen delivery dock," Dylan said upon entering. "This is your last chance, *compadre.*"

"That's a helluva thing for the best man to say." But Jonas grinned as he hugged his friend. Like Jonas's, Dylan's tuxedo was gray and he hoped he looked half as dashing as the judge did. "How much longer before we head for the church?"

"Now—otherwise you'll see the bride, because her limo has arrived as well."

"Alyx was right, we should have eloped."

"Come on, before Parke comes over herself and throws you down the elevator shaft for holding things up. That woman is more excited than E.D. to see this happen."

"Is Blake already there?"

"With the Freemans, yes."

Jonas was proud that his son honored him by agreeing to fly out for the wedding. His teenager had visited once already and had met Alyx and the Freemans. Although he'd been literally openmouthed in his admiration of his stepmother-to-be, Blake was starstruck by H and they'd been talking computers and software ever since his arrival yesterday.

They'd chosen a small chapel to offset the huge reception that would follow. As he and Dylan arrived, he saw all of the people he'd come to know and care for since retiring from the Bureau, and he was especially touched that the Freemans were there in the front pew. Jonas spotted the two guards he'd already hired to watch over them discreetly posted. He paused to hug his son sitting beside H, and shook H's hand. He then stepped across the aisle to kiss E.D., ever-gorgeous and in pink, surrounded by the well-scrubbed Justiss clan.

"Your hands are like ice," she whispered to him.

"My knees are knocking, too. How's she doing?"

"Like you, a wreck."

Most of the others already seated were friends and close associates from Alyx's world of law, and then there were the VIPs, such as the mayor and the governor, sitting right behind the Freemans.

He went back to shake hands with the minister of H and Sarah's Methodist church and then heard the music change, the sign that the bridal party had arrived.

Suddenly the nerves were gone and Jonas nodded calmly and followed the minister out to meet his bride.

Alyx had decided she would walk down the aisle by herself, with Parke leading. His about-to-be-cousin-in-law was a knockout in a seafoam-green silk gown that made her Celtic coloring all the more exotic and had many a male eye follow her hungrily. Then he saw Alyx. Some wreck.

She was a dream in liquid silk, not white, not silver, but

all the radiance of the sun and moon. The gown enhanced her exquisite figure, yet shielded her in all of the places she preferred. Her veil was elegant but modest, and her bouquet was a gentle wave of white roses that finished the illusion of a goddess come to earth.

He took an eager step forward to meet her, a move that brought several chuckles from the pews. Then he and Alyx looked deeply into each other's eyes and everything else and everyone else fell away, and vows were a mere formality.

When Alyx finally managed to maneuver herself and her gown into the limousine for the ride back to the hotel, she sighed in relief and as soon as Jonas settled beside her, she reached for his hand.

"Husband."

"Beloved wife."

They kissed for real this time and when they parted, he suggested, "Let's skip the party?"

Alyx laughed. "The governor wants to make an appearance. Elections are coming up soon and he's hunting donors. And Parke wants you to introduce her to one of your security people, don't ask which because she can only describe him by, um, dimension."

"Soon to be ex-security person if he so much as considers accepting what she has to offer." Jonas shook his head, unable to stop looking at her. "Mrs. Hunter."

"Oh, Jonas, I am so happy."

"And so beautiful." Jonas stared down at her diamond bands and grew serious. "Thank you for all this. I know it's been an ordeal. Will be an ordeal."

"An adventure. One we'll experience together."

He smiled wryly. "You won't let me be serious, will you?"

She stroked his lips with her index finger. "Tonight, my love, you can get as serious as you want…in our bedroom. But first let's go say thank you to all the people who made this possible."

As his imagination started spinning, he grinned. "Then let's party, Mrs. Hunter."

* * * * *

Rufus, as Crystal Hayes had decided to call the black Lab, slept soundly on the soft seat even as she maneuvered the Softco truck in front of the Dean Grosso garage. Engines fired through the open bay doors, compressors clacked and impact tools whined as the teams tweaked their race cars in preparation for qualifying at the third race in Charlotte.

As always when she visited the garage area, Crystal experienced a vicarious thrill, watching the technicians' meticulous, last-minute preparations. As the daughter of a machinist, she understood the difference a fraction of a degree or a thousandth of an inch could make in the performance of a race car.

She muscled the driver's door shut behind her and waved hello to a couple of familiar crew members in their white-and-pale-blue jumpsuits. Then she rounded the back of the truck and rolled up the door. Inside, five boxes were marked Cargill Motors.

One of them was big and heavy, and it had slid forward a few feet, probably when she'd braked to make the narrow parking lot entrance. So she pushed up the sleeves of her canary-yellow T-shirt, then stretched forward to reach the box. A couple of catcalls came her way as her faded blue jeans tightened across her rear end. But she knew they were good-natured, and she simply ignored them.

She dragged the box toward her over the gritty metal floor.

"Let me give you a hand with that," a deep, melodious voice rumbled in her ear.

"I can manage," she responded crisply, not wanting to engage with any of the catcallers.

Here in the garage, the last thing she needed was one of the guys treating her as if she was something other than, well, one of the guys.

She'd learned long ago there was something about her that made men toss out pickup lines like parade candy. And she'd been around race crews long enough to know she needed to behave like a buddy, not a potential date.

She piled the smaller boxes on top of the large one.

"It looks heavy," said the voice.

"I'm tough," she assured him as she scooped the pile into her arms.

He didn't move away, so she turned her head to subject him to a *back off* stare. But she found herself staring into a compelling pair of green…no, brown…no, hazel eyes. She did a double take as they seemed to twinkle, multicolored, under the garage lights.

The man insistently held out his hands for the boxes. There was a dignity in his tone and little crinkles around his eyes that hinted at wisdom. There wasn't a single sign of flirtation in his expression, but Crystal was still cautious.

"You know I'm being paid to move this, right?" she asked him.

"That doesn't mean I can't be a gentleman."

Somebody whistled from a workbench. "Go, Professor Larry."

The man named Larry tossed a "Back off" over his shoulder. Then he turned to Crystal. "Sorry about that."

"Are you for real?" she asked, growing uncomfortable with the attention they were drawing. The last thing she needed was some latter-day Sir Galahad defending her honor at the track.

He quirked a dark eyebrow in a question.

"I mean," she elaborated, "you don't need to worry. I've been fending off the wolves since I was seventeen."

"Doesn't make it right," he countered, attempting to lift the boxes from her hands.

She jerked back. "You're not making it any easier."

He frowned.

"You carry this box, and they start thinking of me as a girl."

Professor Larry dipped his gaze to take in the curves of her figure. "Hate to tell you this," he said, a little twinkle coming into those multifaceted eyes.

Something about his look made her shiver inside. It was a ridiculous reaction. Guys had given her the once-over a million times. She'd learned long ago to ignore it.

"Odds are," Larry continued, a teasing drawl in his tone, "they already have."

She turned pointedly away, boxes in hand as she marched across the floor. She could feel him watching her from behind.

* * * * *

Crystal Hayes could do without her looks,
men obsessed with her looks, and guys who think
they're God's gift to the ladies.
Would Larry be the one guy who could blow all
of Crystal's preconceptions away?
Look for OVERHEATED
by Barbara Dunlop.
On sale July 29, 2008.

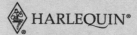

HARLEQUIN®

American ★ Romance®

MARIN THOMAS
A Coal Miner's Wife

HEARTS OF APPALACHIA

High-school dropout and recently widowed
Annie McKee has twin boys to raise. The
now single mom is torn between choosing
charity from her Appalachian clan or leaving
Heather's Hollow and finding a better future
for her boys. But her handsome neighbor and
deceased husband's best friend is determined
to show the proud widow there's nothing
secondhand about love!

**Available August
wherever books are sold.**

LOVE, HOME & HAPPINESS

Harlequin® Historical
Historical Romantic Adventure!

From *USA TODAY*
bestselling author
Margaret Moore

A LOVER'S KISS

A Frenchwoman in London,
Juliette Bergerine is unexpectedly
thrown together in hiding with
Sir Douglas Drury. As lust and
desire give way to deeper emotions,
how will Juliette react on discovering
that her brother was murdered—
by Drury!

*Available September
wherever you buy books.*

HH29508

REQUEST YOUR FREE BOOKS!
2 FREE NOVELS PLUS 2 FREE GIFTS!

Silhouette®

SPECIAL EDITION®

Life, Love and Family!

YES! Please send me 2 FREE Silhouette Special Edition® novels and my 2 FREE gifts (gifts are worth about $10). After receiving them, if I don't wish to receive any more books, I can return the shipping statement marked "cancel." If I don't cancel, I will receive 6 brand-new novels every month and be billed just $4.24 per book in the U.S. or $4.99 per book in Canada, plus 25¢ shipping and handling per book and applicable taxes, if any*. That's a savings of at least 15% off the cover price! I understand that accepting the 2 free books and gifts places me under no obligation to buy anything. I can always return a shipment and cancel at any time. Even if I never buy another book from Silhouette, the two free books and gifts are mine to keep forever.

235 SDN EEYU 335 SDN EEY6

Name _____ (PLEASE PRINT)

Address _____ Apt. #

City _____ State/Prov. _____ Zip/Postal Code

Signature (if under 18, a parent or guardian must sign)

Mail to the **Silhouette Reader Service:**
IN U.S.A.: P.O. Box 1867, Buffalo, NY 14240-1867
IN CANADA: P.O. Box 609, Fort Erie, Ontario L2A 5X3
Not valid to current subscribers of Silhouette Special Edition books.

Want to try two free books from another line?
Call 1-800-873-8635 or visit www.morefreebooks.com.

* Terms and prices subject to change without notice. N.Y. residents add applicable sales tax. Canadian residents will be charged applicable provincial taxes and GST. Offer not valid in Quebec. This offer is limited to one order per household. All orders subject to approval. Credit or debit balances in a customer's account(s) may be offset by any other outstanding balance owed by or to the customer. Please allow 4 to 6 weeks for delivery. Offer available while quantities last.

Your Privacy: Silhouette is committed to protecting your privacy. Our Privacy Policy is available online at www.eHarlequin.com or upon request from the Reader Service. From time to time we make our lists of customers available to reputable third parties who may have a product or service of interest to you. If you would prefer we not share your name and address, please check here. ☐

SSE08R

Inside ROMANCE

Stay up-to-date on all your
romance reading news!

Inside Romance is a FREE quarterly newsletter
highlighting our upcoming series releases
and promotions.

Visit
www.eHarlequin.com/InsideRomance
to sign up to receive our complimentary newsletter today!